AGAINST THE WIND

VIRGINIA KELLY

Dedication

To Bruce, as always

with thanks to:

Ann, Linda, Sheila and Susan,
for their continuing help and support

What others are saying about Virginia Kelly's
Florida Sands Romantic Suspense **series**

"Well written, with a blistering pace, high flying romance and the proverbial fight of good versus evil..." 4.5 Stars. *Tome Tender Book Blog*

"Loved the characters, the plotting, the pacing, the danger around every corner, and I'm sure readers will too." 5 Stars. *Manic Readers*

"Every aspect of the plot was rich and to the point, making this a fast and enjoyable read." 5 Stars, 4 Steam Kettles (*InD'Tale Magazine*)

"Virginia Kelly blends action, romance, and suspense into a fevered frenzy in *Just One Look* and she makes it look easy!" 5 Stars (*Tome Tender Book Blog*)

"excellent twists and turns...will keep readers on the edge of their seats." "*Take a Chance on Me* is an exciting and fast paced book that readers will enjoy." 4 Stars, 4 Steam Kettles (*InDTale Magazine*)

Florida Sands Romantic Suspense

AGAINST THE WIND
JUST ONE LOOK
TAKE A CHANCE ON ME

Chapter One

"Blair."

The sound of Michael's voice saying her name after such a long time stunned her. With the wind howling across the open deck behind him, she grasped the doorknob for balance.

The man she thought she'd never see again stood outlined against the storm-darkened sky. The angles of his body appeared more pronounced, his cheeks leaner, the dark brown eyes she thought she remembered so well, darker.

"Is your grandmother home?" His question skidded along her nerves.

Of course. He and Grandma Alice had kept in touch while Blair hadn't. Couldn't.

Her choice made it impossible.

She forced an answer past her lips. "She's in Europe."

"Are you here to board up?" He shouted to be heard over a sudden gust that lashed at them, precursor

1

of the hurricane churning in the Gulf.

"And to get some of her things."

He braced one hand against the doorframe, close to her shoulder. Several days' growth of beard made him look rough, disreputable. Twin brackets of pain around his mouth startled her.

"Are you okay?"

A smile kicked up one corner of his lips, but didn't reach his eyes. "Just a little sore from an accident."

He glanced over his shoulder, first at the oyster shell drive, then at the sand dune that blocked the view of the crashing surf of the Gulf of Mexico. The wind snatched at a jacket he held folded over his arm. Blair reached out to grasp it, but touched his arm instead, startled at the feel of her fingers on warm flesh. It had been exactly six years.

Not long enough.

He looked at her with an unfathomable expression, then glanced down to where her fingers held his arm. She dropped her hand, remembering she had no right to touch him anymore. "Come in."

He walked past her and lowered himself slowly onto the couch. Very un-Michael like.

Blair shut the door with exaggerated care. She would deal with him, with his mind-numbing reappearance, by focusing only on what she could handle. She would treat him as she would any guest in her grandmother's house. "I think Grandma has some aspirin."

"That'll work." His chest rose and fell with a quick

2

breath. He'd always gone too fast, wanted too much. Lived too hard. And she'd wanted to be with him.

"I'll get it."

Fumbling, Blair managed to get the childproof cap opened. She handed him a glass of water and the tablets.

A gust of wind whipped around the southeast corner of the house, screaming as it tore toward the north and west. Hurricane Nell would visit the barrier island in a few short hours.

Blair twisted her hands together, conscious of her shaky legs. She needed to move, to get away from him. "I have to pack some things and board up the windows." To emphasize her point, she picked up the hammer she'd put down on the coffee table when she'd heard his knock.

"Where's Drew?" Michael's voice sounded harsh.

"He couldn't come. He's on some assignment." Why would he ask about her brother? "You should know the Bureau wouldn't give him any time off to help me."

He took a deep breath and let it out. "So you're alone?"

"Yes."

He stood and walked toward her, his face pale, the man she'd known hidden behind the cool stranger he'd become. "Let me do it, Blair."

From the looks of him, she shouldn't. But no one ever told Michael Alvarez what to do. At least she never had, so she handed him the hammer, explained where the plywood was kept, and watched him don his jacket

3

and walk out into the wind.

Blair wanted to call him back and ask why he was here, but she couldn't force the words past her lips. It didn't matter why he'd come. He was here. She focused on that.

Anything to keep from remembering how things had ended for them. She pulled Grandma Alice's pictures from the walls of each room and took the albums from the living room closet. After packing everything in large, brown plastic bags, Blair turned on the television.

A windblown CNN reporter huddled under a bright yellow rain slicker, microphone to his mouth. "Hurricane Nell, moving over the warm waters of the Gulf of Mexico and heading northwest, is now packing winds of one hundred twenty miles an hour. A mandatory evacuation of low-lying areas and barrier islands along the northwest Florida Gulf Coast has been ordered. Landfall is expected within eight hours." Across the bottom of the screen she read that she and every other beach resident had to leave within two hours.

Blair grabbed the manila folder with her grandmother's important papers and turned off the television. She'd better help Michael. They needed to get off the island soon or they'd be stranded by the rising tide and predicted storm surge.

Wind slammed the front door shut as she pulled the hood of her rain slicker low over her face. While the rain had started only moments ago, it was the wind that bore out the forecast. Blair shouldered her way down the stairs.

She headed toward the back of the house, where she'd heard Michael hammering. The house stood on supportive pilings behind a dune that would protect it from Nell's storm surge. At least Grandma Alice always said the dune had protected her. Watching the wind whip at the sea oats, blowing a haze of sand toward the house, Blair wondered if her grandmother's confidence was justified.

Once down the steps, she walked around her car, curious to know where Michael had parked his. She remembered the Jeep he'd had years ago, the way he loved to drive. Not carelessly, but fast, every ounce of his concentration on the road. Did he still drive that way? Did he still live that way?

As she stepped out from under the protection of the house, sheets of rain, blown off the Gulf by Nell's relentless power, pelted her.

"Michael!" Wind and rain swallowed her words.

Just how bad had his accident been? Had it been a wreck in his Jeep or some speedy sports car? "Michael!" She walked around the end of the house, fighting the force of the storm.

And saw him, lying on the sand, next to a sheet of plywood.

She rushed to his side, letting go of the slicker hood, letting go of the distance she needed to keep between them.

He lay on his right side, hugging his left shoulder.

Even in the muted light of the storm-tossed afternoon, she could see he was pale. "Michael?" Rain pounded her face, blurring her vision.

He jerked his head toward her, eyes squinted against the rain. "My shoulder," he gasped and struggled to sit up, his face a mask of pain. "Wind caught the plywood. Wrenched it from me. Strained my shoulder."

Blair steadied him as he stood, then they stumbled around the house and up the steps. By the time they reached the living room, Michael was shivering so hard his jaws were clenched. He leaned back against the door, eyes closed.

Blair wiped the rain away from her face. Michael looked cold and exhausted. She kicked off her soaked tennis shoes and braced her left shoulder beneath his right arm. "Lean on me."

"I'll knock you over, *niña*."

The endearment he'd used so many times before caught her unaware. "You need to lie down."

He didn't argue, but he didn't let himself relax completely against her, either. They made their way down the hall, Michael's shoes squishing with each step. Once inside the guestroom, she propped him against the wall and squatted down to take off his shoes. Teeth clenched, he helped.

She pulled off his jacket before unbuttoning his soaked, short-sleeved shirt. She'd pulled the shirt out of his jeans, when steely fingers grabbed at her hand.

"No." The word was a hoarse whisper.

"You're wet, Michael. You have to get dry and

6

warm."

He looked at her, his brown eyes wary. His mouth tightened and he released her fingers.

She reached behind him, grimacing when she felt what she thought he was hiding. A gun—a big mean one—in the small of his back. With typical coordination, despite the shivers, Michael pulled it away and held it pointed down.

She pushed the shirt off his shoulders. Her heart skipped a beat when she saw what really concerned him.

The surgical precision of an inches-long scar did not cover the round, red scar one on his left side, above the waist of his jeans. Blair's eyes stung with building tears at the sight of yellow bruising along Michael's ribs, radiating up and out from the wound. A bullet wound. She'd never seen one, but she knew. In Michael's life, it had to be, and explained why he looked so tired, why the accident with the plywood had hurt him so badly. With his help she managed to pull off the shirt.

Shaken, knowing this had been part of her fear all those years ago, she concentrated on the practical—getting him out of his clothes. She struggled with the wet denim, trying to unfasten the single button of his jeans. The zipper was easier, but the wet fabric stuck. Helplessly, she looked up at him, only to see his jaws clenched tighter.

He opened his eyes, so hot, so full of pain, and looked directly at her. "I'm hurt, Blair, not dead." The old Michael would have said the words teasingly. This Michael didn't.

They got the jeans off and he stumbled toward the bed.

Trapped by memory, too aware of reality, Blair indicated his soaked boxers. "Can you—?"

"Turn around. I'll take them off."

Six years and three months ago, she wouldn't have turned away. He wouldn't have asked.

She turned back when she heard him get into the bed and pull up the bedclothes. With exhausted eyes steady on her, he said, "Don't ask questions, Blair."

He hadn't changed. Nothing had changed. She looked down at him. "I wasn't going to."

"I see your questions."

Because she didn't want him to see the feelings she'd kept buried for so long, she moved away. "I'll get a towel for your hair."

The phone rang, shrill and loud, making her jump. She bent to the bedside table and picked up the receiver. "Hello?"

"Blair, are you okay?" Her brother's voice rose over the crackling line.

"Yes, fine." She struggled for words. "Drew, did you—"

She caught Michael's movement. He put his finger to his lips, signaling to her.

He didn't want her brother to know he was here.

"What is it?" Drew's voice pulled her attention back to the phone. "Blair?" He sounded more insistent.

She looked at Michael, at his pale face, at the way he focused on her. "Sorry, connection's bad. I'm almost through boarding up the windows, then I'll leave."

"How bad is the weather?"

"Very windy, rainy. There's a mandatory evacuation."

"Get out." Drew said.

She looked into Michael's eyes, searching for answers. When she didn't find any, she turned away. "I plan to. I'll finish boarding up and grab Grandma's pictures and some papers. Then I'm out of here."

"Good girl."

"I'll talk to you later." A long silence followed her statement. "Drew? You still there?"

"Yeah."

"What's the matter?"

"Do you remember Michael Alvarez?" Drew's question rose over the worsening static on the line.

Blair spun around, her gaze fixed on the man in the bed. "Michael Alvarez?"

Michael shook his head, his dark eyes steady on her.

"Why do you ask?"

"He's—" Drew paused as the line exploded with noise. "I didn't think he'd get in touch with you."

"Why would he?"

The connection popped. Finally, Drew said, "Never mind. Finish up and get out of there. Call me when you get home."

She hung up, never taking her eyes off Michael, and asked, "What's going on?"

Chapter Two

She'd always been a quick study. Michael had loved
watching Blair Davenport's expressive face. Watching—
and wanting—her had been an obsession. Something he
should have fought harder.

Having her for that one week had been heaven.
Losing her, hell.

Coming here and finding her promised to be a
disaster. And if he wasn't careful, they'd both regret this
meeting more than the one six years ago.

Exhausted, he closed his eyes and listened to the
storm. She had every right to expect him to explain, but
he couldn't tell her why Drew was looking for him.
She'd never understand why he'd chosen to hide and
recuperate here, where so much had happened between
them. He didn't understand it himself.

"Well?" Her tone wasn't that of the patient,
somewhat compliant girl she'd been. Had she ever been
compliant? If she had been, wouldn't she have come
with him when he'd asked?

"I'll be out of here after I rest."

"That's not an answer, Michael." She gave him one
of those polite looks he imagined she used on

recalcitrant servants.

"It's the only one I have." He struggled to keep his eyes open.

She studied him, the green of her eyes darker than the raging Gulf. "We still have power. I'll put your clothes into the dryer." She bent, picked up the wet mess from the floor, and walked out.

Already half asleep, Michael watched her leave. The familiarity of her walk, the sway of her hips, reminded him of so much. She wore her sun-streaked dark hair, wet from the rain, in a ponytail. Six years ago she'd worn it down, let him run his hands through it while he—

His body protested the image. With conscious effort he let himself slide into sleep.

* * *

The sound of the wind woke him. Momentarily startled and a little disoriented, he remembered exactly where he was, exactly what had happened.

He was in Alice Davenport's house with Blair, the only woman he'd ever wanted to marry, who'd come into his life at a time when he'd least expected. He could hear her moving around. He sat up, the ache of his month-old wound a persistent throb, a constant reminder of the need to hide. Gingerly, he rotated his left shoulder and found he wasn't as sore as he'd thought he'd be. He stood, relieved that he didn't feel as exhausted, and pulled the sheet around his hips. He considered draping the thing higher across his left side to hide the fresh scar, then discarded the thought as ridiculous. Blair had already seen it.

She came down the hall as Michael tucked the sheet around his waist. She paused in the doorway, her arms full of his clothes, and stared.

He wished he could step into her thoughts, inside

what made her tick. He thought he had, years ago, but he'd been wrong.

"They're dry," she announced, the polite look still firmly in place.

"Thanks," he said, making no move toward her.

She appeared to struggle with herself before stepping into the room. "There's an evacuation order. We have to leave. Someone from the Sheriff's Department should be around to get us out if we don't."

Michael couldn't read her at all anymore. She was a blank page to him. The knowledge he had of her was of a laughing, passionate young woman who'd ripped away the only real hold he had on life in a time of turmoil.

"Do you mind if they see you?"

Yes, she was a quick study. "I'd rather they didn't."

"Then you should leave now."

"No more questions, Blair?"

"Would you answer them if I asked?"

No, not one bit compliant. He wondered why she bothered to ask if he minded if the deputies saw him. "I can't."

"Then get dressed." She dumped his clothes on the bed. "I finished covering the back windows so all we have to do is lock up. Where's your car?"

"I don't have one." It lay submerged in the bay, a sacrifice to expediency. Another fact she would never know.

She seemed to bite back some comment, before saying, "Then you'll come with me."

Blair Davenport had grown up, taken charge. She was twenty-eight now. At twenty-two, she'd wanted simplicity, someone to give her direction, yet freedom. He'd wanted to be the one to see her spread her wings, but—

Hell, Michael wasn't sure what had happened. He

was only sure he'd spent six years cursing the insanity that had prompted him to ask her to marry him.

* * *

Blair leaned back against the door. Despite the weight loss and the marring of his body, Michael Alvarez was still the most attractive man she'd ever seen. She wondered about the women in his life. There had to be at least one. She couldn't imagine Michael's life without women. Even Grandma Alice had succumbed to his charm.

As Blair had so long ago.

Falling in love with Michael had been easy. Letting go, after a week of passion, was harder than anything she'd ever done. She'd survived the loneliness of her refusal to marry him with nothing more than sheer determination and years of struggle. Years of struggle that wouldn't end by giving in to whatever aberration made her so susceptible to him.

She didn't want to deal with those old feelings again. She wouldn't. She'd dried his clothes and she'd see him on his way. That was more than enough.

Back in her grandmother's room, Blair looked around for anything she thought Grandma Alice might want. As she checked the top of the dresser for things she should take, she turned on the radio so she could listen to the hurricane update.

It only confirmed what she knew: Nell would arrive shortly. Then the announcer began a new story. One about a wounded FBI agent sought by the Bureau. Blair stood by the bed, her gaze frozen on the small radio. The story was brief but the upshot was that Michael, in his capacity as a special agent with the Miami office of the FBI, had vanished. He'd walked out of the hospital where he was recuperating from a bullet wound.

Drew hadn't explained, but why would her brother

say anything to her about one of his best friends? Drew knew nothing of what had happened between her and Michael. Not even Grandma Alice knew it all.

Michael had left Miami two weeks ago. The day Grandma Alice left for London. Blair listened intently, trying to read between the lines to see if there was any indication of Michael's status as an undercover agent.

"Blair?"

She jumped at the sound of his voice. Dressed in his dry clothes, Michael stood in the doorway. Their eyes met and held as the announcer finished his story. "All law enforcement officers in the area are on the lookout for Michael Alvarez. He was last seen yesterday, in Emerald Bay."

Blair turned off the radio. "You should have stayed in the hospital."

Cool eyes regarded hers. "If I had, I'd be a dead man now."

That was the most Michael had ever said to her about his work. The most he'd ever revealed.

"Does Drew know?"

Michael paused, his eyes narrowed. "He thinks he does."

"Meaning?"

"The less you know the better."

"I'm not the girl I was years ago, Michael."

"No, you're not. But I'm a man with a target on my back."

"You thought the house would be empty, didn't you?"

"I know Alice goes to London this time of year."

"You can't hide with a hurricane coming."

"Best place to hide."

"Nell's a category three. The house won't be here."

Pounding on the door made her jump. She looked at

14

Michael. He stood straight and tall, so alert he looked bigger.

She broke the hold of his eyes. "Coming!" she shouted, and made her way to the living room. Fumbling into the yellow rain slicker, she grabbed the bag full of framed pictures. Out of the corner of her eye, she saw Michael retreat into the bedroom.

She pulled the front door open, expecting to see a deputy, and felt the rush of wind and rain.

It wasn't anyone from the Sheriff's Department.

"Yes?" she shouted against the roar of the storm.

"Sorry to disturb you," said a heavyset man wrapped in a blue rain slicker. "I'm looking for a friend who rode down here with me to look at the storm."

"What?" She'd heard him, but had given herself a chance to think, to study the stranger.

"Looking for a friend," he shouted. "Tall, dark hair. Seen anyone like that?"

"No!" The word seemed to be sucked away by Nell's force.

Lights from a deputy's cruiser flashed through the rain as it approached the house.

"Maybe the deputy has seen your friend," Blair shouted. She pulled the door shut behind her and made her way down the stairs.

She couldn't hear if the stranger said anything to the deputy. It looked like they only nodded in passing.

"You leavin' soon, ma'am?" a young deputy she didn't know asked as he pulled up near the house.

"I need to get one more thing from the house. This storm is really bad, isn't it?"

"Yes, ma'am, sure is. These are just the outlying bands. Toll bridge across the bay is already out. You'll have to take the one out toward High Point." Rain pelted the deputy's face through the open cruiser window. "How far are you going?"

"I'm from Emerald Bay, but I thought I'd drive north, toward Atlanta."

"I hear hotels are fillin' up quick. You might have some trouble." He pointed at the boarded windows. "You do that by yourself?"

"I, ah, had some help."

"Well, be careful drivin' now." He shifted gears, then shouted, "Listen to the radio. There's a shelter up toward High Point, at the elementary school, if you get caught."

She thanked the deputy, threw the bags in the trunk of her car, and went back upstairs. She shook the rain slicker as she stepped inside.

Michael stood to one side looking out through a crack in the boarded kitchen window. "What did he want?"

"Just to be sure I'm leaving."

"I mean the other man."

She wanted to see his reaction, see if he would explain. "He wants you."

Michael didn't even glance at her. He watched out the boarded window. Blair imagined he could see the stranger and the deputy slowly drive away toward the county road.

"We need to go," she said.

"You go on." Michael continued to look out. "Be careful."

Even if he'd taken leave of his senses, she couldn't abandon him to ride out a category three hurricane. She couldn't leave anyone to that fate. "You can't stay here." She sounded more like she was speaking to her eighteen kindergarten students than to a grown man.

"I can't leave." Now he did look at her, those dark eyes intense, but still cool.

"It's likely the house won't make it."

"I'll risk it."

His statement sounded so ridiculous that she blurted, "Get real." A quick breath calmed her and she continued. "I have a car. I'm going as far as I can."

"You're not going far enough for me."

That gave her pause. Torn between the need to protect herself and some other undefined feeling, she managed, "I will." There. She'd said it.

That the words were those he'd expected six years earlier wasn't wasted on Michael. She read the surprise on his face.

"Bad timing, Blair."

"You can't stay here."

"Blair—"

"Be reasonable. We'll get in the car and go. That man was looking for you, he probably knows you're here. He'll think you stayed." She wouldn't plead. She shouldn't care. "It makes sense to leave."

Michael moved toward her, away from the window. Blair took in the sensuous mouth, the beard-roughened jaw, and the amazing eyes. The way his body moved. This was the man she'd said no to.

"Go get in your car, Blair," he said, standing before her.

Blair felt his nearness, the heat from his body. For a single moment she thought he might touch her cheek, but he never raised his arm.

"Don't second guess good sense," he said. "You made the right choice years ago."

* * *

Michael watched her leave, Nell's hurricane-force winds pulling at her bright yellow slicker. She put some more of Alice's things in the trunk of her silver Toyota and, with one last glance toward the kitchen window where he stood, walked around to the driver's side of her car.

That's when Michael saw him. Hiding behind a supporting piling, ready to make his move. A month ago, he wouldn't have hesitated to burst out of the door, pistol drawn. Today, with Blair in the way and exhaustion lingering despite his nap, he waited a fraction of a second too long. A single shot would have taken the man out and rendered Blair safe. But it was too late.

He saw Blair turn, saw her body stiffen as she took in the sight of the stranger holding a .357 on her. The man mouthed directions at her, the revolver aimed straight at her chest.

* * *

Blair released her grip on the car door and stepped away. As ordered. Shock kept her from being afraid, from real understanding. The gun looked huge.

"Come here!" the man who'd come looking for Michael shouted.

She did as she was told, praying her legs wouldn't buckle as she rounded the car.

"Where's the old lady who owns this place?"

"London."

"When'd she leave?"

"A couple of weeks ago."

A vivid curse erupted from the man's mouth. He fumbled in the pocket of his raincoat and pulled out a cell phone. After punching buttons, he shouted, "Eddie!" He listened briefly, glanced down at the phone, and muttered "damn it" before shoving it in his pocket.

"The deputy will be back," Blair said, praying the man would leave now that he couldn't communicate with anyone.

"Go down the driveway to my car," he ordered. The

gun he held still loomed large, but he'd dropped it a bit, apparently confused by his inability to get in touch with Eddie.

She couldn't do as he said. But she couldn't run. He'd shoot her.

He was going to shoot her anyway. She felt the bite of the car keys in her hand and reason fled. She threw the keys at the man's face. Instinctively, he brought both hands up to protect his eyes, the momentarily forgotten gun hitting his right cheek.

Just as she turned to run, she saw a flash of movement, an emerging shape, from behind the man.

Michael made a quick motion and the stranger fell heavily.

"Damn, Blair." Michael, his breath too quick, bent to check the man's neck. "That's the dumbest thing I've ever seen. How were you going to drive away?"

Michael pulled the gun from the man's limp fingers, rolled him onto his back, and searched his pockets.

"I didn't have time to think." A gust of wind cut through her, making her shiver despite its warmth.

He pulled the man's wallet out and rifled through the contents. "Aw, hell." He threw the wallet down on the concrete carport.

"What is it?"

"Fake IDs."

"Oh," she replied, as if hearing that someone carried fake IDs was an every day occurrence.

He picked up the keys from the cement. "Let's go," he said handing them to her. He checked the gun.

"You're coming with me?"

He looked down at the unconscious man while putting the gun into the back waistband of his jeans. "You're right. I can't stay here. Drive me across the bay and leave me."

"How will you get away?"

He shouted over the sound of the wind. "Let's just go before this guy wakes and Nell blows us away."

* * *

The county road was nearly impassible. Wind whipped at the low-growing scrub oaks, rain slashed across the road in front of them. The overworked wipers struggled against the deluge. Michael wished he was driving, but he had to look out for Eddie and company. He wondered which side of the game Eddie fell on. The good guys or the bad. Or the ones in between.

Blair's white-knuckled grip on the wheel made him curse himself for the fool he was. No, he couldn't go to his family, they were being watched. But what had made him run into a hurricane? To a place where Blair filled the memories he still tried to avoid?

"Michael," she said, breaking into his thoughts, "there's a road block up ahead."

Cruiser lights flashed fifty yards down the road. It was too late to turn back. "Keep going. If they stop us, come to a complete stop. I'm your friend, Kevin Johnson, from Atlanta."

He hid his Glock beneath the folds of the rain slicker he'd taken from Alice's. The .357 went beneath the seat.

At the roadblock, Michael watched a tall man in a Sheriff's Department-issue rain slicker approach Blair's side of the car. Rain slashed in when she rolled down her window.

The deputy leaned down. "Blair," he said in a friendly shout, "I wondered who was going to board up Miss Alice's windows."

"I, uh, came over this morning, Charlie." Blair's discomfort was palpable.

Charlie held his rain hood over his head. "Go on up

to High Point. It's the only way off the island." He peered at Michael.

"Charlie, this is ... ah, Kevin." Blair gripped the steering wheel harder. "From Atlanta." She would make a rotten actress.

"Kevin." Charlie nodded a hello. He straightened slightly and spoke to Blair again. "Glad you brought someone with you. Seems somebody's gotten away from some FBI fellas. They got the crazy idea the guy's down here hiding. Can you believe that? What fool would come down here to hide in this mess?" Charlie laughed, then backed away from the car. "Go on, now, and be careful."

Blair began rolling her window up. "Thanks, Charlie." Back on the road, the sound of the wipers nearly drowned out her next words. "It was dumb to think you could hide here."

Michael smiled. How many times during that one incredible week had Blair bitten her tongue to keep from saying what was on her mind? "About as dumb as throwing your car keys at a guy who's holding a gun on you."

It took forty-five minutes to get to High Point, a resort village on the east end of the island. The drive normally took fifteen. One other car had dared the drive, one with Mississippi tags. Blair said it belonged to some people who lived two houses down from Alice. The couple stopped and spoke to the deputies manning the roadblock at the bridge.

Michael saw one deputy point back down the road and knew they were too late. They'd be riding Nell out on the island. He told Blair to go ahead and pull up to the deputies.

"Middle span of the bridge is gone!" the young man shouted, his face dripping rain. "Runaway barge hit it.

Westside bridge is closed because it's so low the water's washing over it." He ran a hand down his face, wiping away water. "Best thing to do is head for the elementary school. Go back the way you came and take the first right."

Hands tight on the wheel, her mouth set in a straight line, Blair thanked the deputy. Michael hoped the young officer would believe she looked tense because of the hurricane, not because of the man sitting in her car.

As they pulled away, Michael said, "You should have left while I was sleeping."

She threw him a quick glance, then concentrated on the road. "And leave you to die?"

She didn't know how likely that was to happen anyway. And if she was with him when they caught him, how likely it was to happen to her, too.

"How safe's this school going to be?" he asked.

"It's closer to the bay side, so it should be okay. Grandma rode out a smaller storm there a couple of years ago."

But Alice hadn't had half the country looking for her.

"I'm still Kevin Johnson from Atlanta," Michael reminded. If they weren't careful, her nerves would give away his identity.

"You don't look like a Kevin."

"No, I look like Miguel." His quick reply surprised him and made him sound thin-skinned. Miguel was his real name, the Anglicized Michael something he accepted as the price of coming from Argentina to the States at the age of fifteen. Except for the last thing he'd said to her a lifetime ago, he'd never put in to words what had lurked at the back of his consciousness from the moment he met Blair Davenport.

"That's not what I meant," Blair threw him a quick look.

22

So she remembered what he'd said and didn't like it. But it had been the thought of dragging home a Latino boyfriend that made her change her mind after only one week. Fair-haired Blair Davenport of the Virginia Davenports thought she'd been slumming.

"Kevin is too soft a name for you."

Determined to cut off memories best forgotten, he injected humor into his voice. "Would Lance suit me better?"

Her body relaxed a bit. "That's a horrible name for you." She kept a firm grip on the wheel, her eyes on the road. "Michael is who you are. Michael and whatever the mysterious middle A stands for."

He thought of all the intimacies they'd shared and of those things they hadn't, like his middle name. Which made him wonder again what had possessed his very American mother to give him such an un–American name. One that, in its simplicity, made him Latin American to the core.

"Here we are," she said.

The school, built of cinder block and painted beige, was probably twenty years old. A few cars were parked close to the front doors. No way to know who was inside.

Once Blair parked, Michael shifted in the seat and put the Glock in the back waistband of his jeans. When he straightened, Blair was staring at him, her eyes wide.

"You're not taking that in, are you?"

"I'll need it if Eddie's in there."

She took that in quietly. "What if you told the deputies what's going on?"

"Blair," he said patiently, "I've told people who trust me and they don't believe me. What makes you think a total stranger would?"

"Drew doesn't believe you?"

She was a very quick study. "I haven't spoken to him."

"He's your friend."

"He's an FBI agent. First and foremost."

"He wouldn't let anybody hurt you."

"I've already been hurt. Hurt's not what somebody wants to do to me."

A gust of wind shook the car. "Oh."

"We'd better go in. You taking your bag?" he asked, pointing to the back seat.

"Yes." She started to reach for the bag, a backpack she'd chosen for its convenience, but he grabbed it first. He placed the other gun, the one he'd gotten from the man at the house, inside.

Michael reached for the door handle and felt her hand on his arm.

"I'm probably going to know some of these people. Let me do the talking, okay?"

He nodded and they both made a run for the front of the school.

"Blair!"

She turned in the process of pulling open the door. A deputy approached from one side of the protective overhang.

"Evan, what are you doing here?" With a too-quick movement, she leaned toward the blond-haired man and hugged him.

"I was helping with the evacuation. Becky said she saw you at the school."

"I did what I could there this morning. Virgil couldn't board up Grandma's house because his wife was sick, so I came over." She shot Michael a quick look. He hoped Evan wouldn't pick up on how nervous she was.

Evan nodded and looked past Blair at Michael.

"Who's your friend?"

Blair spun around, eyes wide. "Oh, Evan, this is, ah … Kevin Johnson. Kevin, Evan Chambers, my best friend's husband."

"Nice to meet you." Evan smiled, extending his hand. "What brings you to Saint's Island in the middle of a hurricane?"

Before Michael could say anything, Blair spoke. "He came to help me because—"

If he'd been thinking faster, he could have stopped her. Maybe.

"He's … ah … we're engaged."

Chapter Three

It wasn't a Freudian slip, Blair told herself. She hadn't meant to say it, hadn't secretly wished for it all these years. She couldn't still want a man who refused to trust her with his secrets.

Evan looked surprised, but he hugged her and congratulated Michael, shaking his hand. Michael took it all in stride. Now, as they walked down one of the empty school hallways, Blair sucked in a quick breath, trying to calm herself.

"You don't think well under pressure, do you?"

Michael's words didn't help. "If you mean I don't lie well, then no, I don't." She hated sounding defensive. "I suppose you could have done better on the spur of the moment."

"I wouldn't have dug a pit we're going to have a hell of a time getting out of," he said, pulling her along, looking back over his shoulder.

She stopped, forcing him to face her. "Evan was staring at you."

"He was looking at me. We were being introduced."

She should have said nothing. She should never have offered to help him. "I can't do this, Michael."

A long, patient sigh was his only response.

It made her angry. "I'm doing the best I can."

He watched her for a moment. "You are, Blair, and I appreciate it." The soft rumble of his voice broke the tension. She remembered why they were here, like this. Why she was willing to risk spending any time with Michael. "I'll do what I said. I'll take you as far as I can."

"That's—"

"It's so wonderful to see you, Blair, and to hear your wonderful news!" A woman's high-pitched voice broke in.

Bitsy Caldwell, an old friend of Grandma Alice's, came toward them, beaming. Blair forced a smile, knowing she'd have to lie again. "Mrs. Caldwell, how are you?" Blair asked, hugging the older woman.

"Call me Bitsy, honey, please. I'm fine, just fine. Evan says you're engaged to this nice young man." Mrs. Caldwell—Bitsy—had what Grandma Alice called a *joie de vivre*. Blair had always thought of her as an unrepentant flirt, to put it mildly. She batted her eyelashes and primped as she extended her hand toward Michael.

"Mrs. Caldwell," he replied in that deep, steel-melting voice, shaking her hand. If Bitsy had been thirty years younger, she would have thrown herself at him. Right then she looked as if she might do so despite her age.

"Bitsy, I insist," she replied, with a flirtatious smile.

"Oh, my, Blair." The older woman released Michael's hand reluctantly and held her own hand to her well displayed cleavage. "Why didn't Alice tell me you were engaged?"

Blair's thoughts froze.

Michael broke the long, empty silence. "I just popped the question today."

"How wonderful! This calls for a celebration."

Mobilized by the possible consequences of a party, Blair reached out to touch Bitsy's arm. "That's not—"

"I don't think—" Michael protested.

"Nonsense. We're stuck here at least until the morning. Let's have a party!" Bitsy hurried away. From the slight tilt to her walk, Blair suspected Bitsy had already partied. Over her shoulder she shouted, "Don't worry about a thing!"

Blair mentally kicked herself and the insanity of a fictitious engagement. She'd never be able to pull off such a thing. From the moment she'd opened the front door to Michael, she'd been fighting the urge to run. If it hadn't been for Nell, she would have.

That was crazy. She couldn't have left him in the path of a hurricane.

She couldn't deal with any of this. Desperate to do something, anything, Blair turned toward Michael, intent on asking what they would tell all these people.

But Michael wasn't paying attention to her. He was looking down the hall at Evan, who called, "Blair, the man in charge of the shelter wants you to register. Come on down here."

"What'll we do?" Blair whispered.

"Register?" Michael whispered back.

She stopped and stared at him. "This isn't funny."

"I don't think it is." He signaled Evan they were coming and the other man walked away.

"Then quit acting like it."

"Blair," Michael said quietly. "Not a damn thing about this mess is funny." He put his hands on her shoulders and bent toward her, forcing her to look up at him. "It's my fault your friend is throwing us a party. Hell, it's my fault we're here." He paused, his attention directed solely at her. "But it'll be okay by tomorrow. By then I'll be out of your life for good. Everything will be fine."

She shouldn't care; she didn't want to care. But

mostly she hated that she couldn't stop her question. "Will you be fine?"

He dropped his hands from her shoulders, giving her back some of the distance she craved. "Don't worry about it. It's not your concern."

The words felt like a slap on the face. "You made it my concern by coming here."

He looked down at her, his thoughts hidden, his expression unreadable.

"You should call Drew," she said.

He said nothing for a moment. "Let's get through Nell. Then I'll worry about Drew."

* * *

There were sixteen people in all, including four deputies. Michael didn't like the idea that they wore their Magnums on their hips while his Glock wasn't as handy in the small of his back. But of the group of sixteen people, all, except the deputies, were part of a couple. Eddie and company would not be traveling with their wives.

An army chopper pilot had his hands full dealing with his two-year-old. While the little boy wiggled and squirmed, the wife ran to the bathroom at least five times in the span of an hour. Michael hoped she wouldn't give whatever she had to the rest of them.

Bitsy Caldwell did throw a party. While Nell roared outside and news of the storm came in double doses from two radios, Michael and Blair were toasted with soda from paper cups. Bitsy, Michael was sure, had something a bit stronger in her enormous purse, because she grew increasingly merry.

Blair sat cross-legged on a blanket laughing at the impromptu jingles sung for their benefit. Michael couldn't help but wonder what it would have been like if she hadn't refused him all those years ago. If he were now married to Blair. And he felt her unease when Bitsy, in her alcohol-induced speech, wished them beautiful children.

Beautiful children. Damn.

He clearly remembered the words he'd thrown at Blair that last morning, remembered the deep, smoky hurt in her eyes. He'd spent six years excusing himself with the knowledge that she hadn't wanted a future with him.

The power went off at about ten, throwing them into darkness. A flashlight, one with a fluorescent bulb, provided their light. They all sat huddled on blankets and chairs, their backs against the cold brick walls, while Nell pounded away at their refuge. Periodically, they could hear debris hitting the building.

As Nell howled around them, Michael wondered about the man at Alice's. He'd either found shelter or he was dead.

Finally, the crackling radios were turned down. An hour of listening to the wind and the strange noises it made, quieted the room. The pilot's wife quit making her dashed forays into the bathroom, and their little boy slept on a pile of blankets.

The ache in Michael's side and shoulder made sleep impossible. That and the fact that he lay next to Blair, wondering how in the hell he'd managed to get her involved in this mess, how he'd managed to screw things up so badly before.

Until Blair, he'd lived with the sure knowledge that if he worked hard enough, he would always get what he wanted. He'd gotten a chance to avenge his brother, but he'd lost Blair. That failure had colored his life in the years that followed. The visits he'd made to his family, pretending all was well, only worried them, and not just because of the dangers of his job. Hell, he'd worried himself. He expected—needed—some degree of normalcy, at least in his private life. Blair had been his chance at that life.

Had the search for that, for her, brought him here? If that were true, then he was a much bigger fool than he'd thought. Because what moneyed Blair Davenport considered a normal life was a million miles from his normal.

In an effort to relax, he rotated his shoulder, trying to ease the aching stiffness, and lay down. Blair lay stretched out on her side next to him.

The next thing he knew, he was having the most incredibly erotic dream. About Blair. Only it wasn't a dream, it was a replay of that single week. He woke lying on his right side, spooned against Blair, his left hand low on her stomach. He was so close he could smell her sweetness, feel her hair against his face.

If he was this close, then she could feel him. He tried to ease away when every male instinct screamed at him to pull her closer, to reach up and feel the soft weight of her breasts in his palm. He managed to shift slightly, only to have her move with him. She scooted her behind against his lap, making him groan in the darkness of the hall.

She woke, startled, and sat up, turning to look down at him in the dim light, her beautiful eyes wide, her hair tousled. And he wanted her, just like he'd wanted her six years ago.

No. More. Because the wanting was now steeped in memory, in things better left forgotten.

"I'm sorry," she said, her voice rough from sleep. She pushed her hair back with one hand.

"I didn't mean—"

"I didn't think—"

They spoke in unison.

Michael cleared his throat and sat up. Darkness would conceal his condition, but he was uncomfortable as hell in his jeans. Memories flooded him, making him want to drag Blair down to the blanket. "I, ah, wasn't thinking."

"It's okay." The sleepy quality of her voice agitated his nerve endings.

It was too much. He'd wanted too much then, he wanted it now. Now, when it was more impossible than before. He had to walk away, as she had long ago. "I'm going to take a look outside."

The night was wilder than anything he'd ever seen. An eerie glow provided just enough contrast to make out shapes. Nell had ripped the big oak in front of the school out of the ground. Michael peered through small windows in the double door at the wind-sheered darkness and saw the outlines of the cars. They'd been shoved together. There would be dents and scratches, but at least they were still there.

He heard footsteps in the hall and turned.

"Cars still out there?" the pilot asked, looking out.

"Barely."

"One hell of a blow."

They stood in silence, watching.

"Deputy Chambers says the eye has moved west. They think it's going into Mississippi," the pilot said.

"Glad we didn't get that, but this side of the storm's been bad enough."

"You're damn right."

"How's your wife?"

The pilot turned toward him. "She's pregnant."

"Congratulations."

"She's not happy."

Damn, but this was uncomfortable. "Oh."

"We've always wanted more kids." Michael saw him

run a hand through his short hair. "But I'm shipping out and she can't come. She'll have this one alone."

"That's rough."

"Tell me about it. Her family never wanted her to marry an army man and now I'm leaving. They won't help."

"What about yours?"

"My mother works. She'll come down for a week or two, but that's all she can manage."

In silence, they watched the ripping wind.

"You and Blair planning on having children?"

Michael felt something inside give. "Yes." He'd wanted children with Blair six years ago. She didn't even want him long enough to listen.

"What do you do?"

The lie came too easily. "I'm an accountant."

"Good. Nice stable job. That's what you need for a family. The army's been my life, but the multiple deployments are too much if you want a sane family life. I'm getting out as soon as I can."

"What about flying?"

The pilot shook his head. "It's one of those things. I can't have both."

Long minutes after the pilot had left, Michael thought about what he'd said. Michael had wanted it all: Blair and the job.

He'd wound up with neither.

* * *

Blair turned fitfully on the scratchy blanket. Everyone was asleep. Everyone except Michael. And her.

She'd spent six years and three months coming to terms with Michael's refusal to explain anything, with the burning need in him for something she couldn't understand. His last words replayed themselves on bad nights. On good nights, she could push aside the lingering memories and doubts. She didn't need a man with too many secrets, who kept so much of himself inside. A man who promised a life made up of quick visits home before he had to leave again.

Blair had seen what that did to two people. Her father had bull dozed his way in to her mother's life, determined to have her, unaware that she could not cope with his wealthy life-style, with the gap between their expectations of married life. In the end they'd led separate lives, with a few weeks each year together. Those weeks and their children were their only connection to the love they bore for each other.

Blair refused to replay her parents' relationship. She wanted one based on trust and sharing. One Michael couldn't provide.

But the reality was that seeing Michael again made her question her resolve. What if she hadn't said no? What if she'd been with him for the last six years? Would she also have the satisfaction of knowing she had touched so many lives? Or would marrying him have ruled out what she'd built for herself? A life full of giggling voices turning to her with small eager arms raised saying, "I know, Miss Davenport!"

Without Michael, she had only to worry about her school, about the classroom windows she'd boarded up in an attempt to protect them from Nell's wrath. About the materials she'd accumulated in her years at Emerald Bay Elementary, about small hands clutching hers. Listening to the wind told her how vulnerable all she'd worked for really was. One gust could destroy her careful planning, leaving her classroom nothing but an empty place.

Just as this meeting with Michael would leave her. Empty and wondering. Again.

Because Michael was still Michael. He was older, harder somehow. And she was just as helpless to fight the overwhelming attraction as she'd been then. He hadn't needed her then, had shut her out of everything about his life. Only when they'd made love had she felt she was touching his soul. That was the memory that tantalized her.

He strode up the dimly lit hallway. Tall and graceful. So male. He sat down next to her, his back against the wall.

Desperate to distance herself from the feelings that threatened to overwhelm her, she asked, "What's it like outside?"

"Calming down now, but it was bad."

"How's my car?"

He hesitated. "We won't be able to get to it right away. It's mashed up against the others."

"How will we get away?"

She saw the flash of his teeth against his smile. That smile she'd almost forgotten. "You're a gutsy babe, Blair Davenport."

"I'm not a babe at all." She laughed at his choice of words and at her prudish sounding response. "I thought we might get across the other bridge when the water goes down."

He laughed softly. "You're a lady with a practical streak."

This time she read the admiration in his voice. It pierced a hidden place in her heart. "How will we do it?"

"A tenacious lady with a practical streak," he corrected.

Blair looked around the hallway to make sure no one was awake. "Michael, you have to get away."

He bowed his head. The dim light reflected off his

hair. "Let's worry about that in the morning."

She wanted answers. She'd wanted them from the moment she saw him standing in Grandma Alice's doorway, had to know if he'd changed enough to give them to her. "What happened?"

"It's long and complicated."

"Nell won't let us out."

"No, she won't." He sounded resigned, tired.

"Who's after you?"

He laughed at that, but this laugh was harsh. "Everybody."

"Drew?"

He hesitated. "Yes."

She shook her head. "Not Drew. He knows you."

"It looks bad, Blair. I screwed up. I missed something big, trusted where I shouldn't trust."

"Eddie and his friend?"

"I don't know whose side they fall on. Could be the Bureau could be the bad guys."

She thought about that for a moment. "You have to fix this."

"No basic questions, Blair? No, 'what did you do wrong, Michael?'"

"No." That should have surprised her. It surprised her more that it didn't.

"Even after what hap—"

"I should have …" She struggled for the words, but only one explanation came to mind. "It wasn't meant to be."

He sat up straighter and reached out toward her. The contact of his fingers on her cheek felt charged. "We had something, Blair. Something—"

A roaring caught their attention, before the rapid change in pressure.

"Tornado!" A man's yell came from the other end of

the hall. "Get down!"

Blair felt the weight of Michael's body as he pushed her down on the rough blanket and pulled her beneath him. The noise intensified until it was deafening. Above the roar came other sounds. Metal crashing, a shuddering throughout the building. Shattering sounds came from behind the wall at their heads. It seemed to go on forever.

Then it was quiet. Too quiet.

The two-year-old began crying, softly at first, then with increasing urgency. His mother crooned to him.

Around them, people began shifting. Above Blair, Michael moved, hesitated, then pushed away. With the feel of his body echoing through her, Blair sat up. The couple next to them turned up their flashlight. In the harsh light, Michael's features were pinched. Flat on his back, he ran his hand from shoulder to chest.

Blair scooted closer. "What can I do?"

"I'll be okay," he said between gritted teeth.

Evan came down the hall, checking on everyone. When he reached them, he asked, "Kevin, you okay?"

Michael replied. "Wrenched my shoulder. It'll be all right."

Evan nodded and moved on. Once he'd checked on everybody, gone to the front of the hall and come back, he turned to the huddled group. "We'll wait until light to try to leave. It looks pretty bad. The cars are ruined. I'm going to try to get hold of my dispatcher and see if we can't have a boat sent to get us once the waters calm down."

* * *

The first light of day found them all gathered outside the front of the schoolhouse. The cars, which Michael knew had sustained some damage from the hurricane force winds, now lay on their sides or on their roofs, some on top of each other, as if a great wreck had destroyed them. Blair's car lay on top of a red one.

"Did you get in touch with anybody?" the pilot asked Evan, shifting his two-year-old to his other arm.

"Yeah. They're sending a couple of boats out. We'll have to walk down to Baker's Landing where we'll gather with some folks from the church. They're afraid to put in by the bridge because of the debris and all."

"How far's the landing?" the pilot's wife asked.

"About a mile or so."

"That's not far," Bitsy Caldwell said with a smile. She looked none the worse for wear from her extended celebrating.

A little after eight, the small group followed the deputies around and behind the school along an oyster shell road that led to the edge of the bay. Michael carried Blair's bag and felt the reassuring weight of the Glock in the small of his back. All around them, palm fronds, broken tree limbs, pink housing insulation, and pieces, both large and small, of signs and houses covered the ground.

As they made their way over the debris, their shoes making crunching sounds on the oyster shells, Blair asked, "Are you okay?"

"A little sore."

"There are a couple more aspirin."

"I took some. I'll be all right." He realized he'd cut her off too quickly. "How are you? I mean, did you get any rest last night?"

She looked up at him with those fabulous green eyes. "On and off. I couldn't get the picture of that man at the house out of my mind."

"Don't think about him, *niña*, you handled him well."

"You said it was dumb to throw—"

"You scared me. I reacted." He regretted the words

immediately. They proved he still cared. He couldn't afford the luxury. "Tell me about yourself. What you're doing now."

She looked back at him. "I teach kindergarten here in Emerald Bay."

He knew, of course. Drew had told him. And though Drew didn't know about the endless week they'd spent together, he had spoken about his family. Michael soaked up every word about Blair. Every word. Including the news that she was engaged to some fool who couldn't have known what to do with her. She'd broken that engagement.

But it was Alice who had filled in the gaps, who told him about the Blair he remembered. About her spirit. And made him ache in the wanting of all that was Blair.

"I may move up to the first grade next year." A strong steady breeze pushed at her hair. She'd braided it last night but hadn't bothered this morning, wearing a ponytail bound with one of those cloth things—a red one.

They reached the place where the deputies said the boats would pick them up. In the distance, a group of thirteen people walked toward them from the opposite direction. Michael studied their faces as they drew nearer. Two couples, each with two children, one park ranger, still in his uniform, and four women around sixty-five. Behind them walked a lone man wearing a suit. Not the one who'd looked for him at Alice's house. Eddie, maybe?

Three felled oaks gave them a place to sit as they waited. By the time the other group of people joined them, two Marine Patrol boats were cutting across the sun-glinted bay, two officers on each boat.

"Michael?" Blair's question was soft, as quiet as a breath. "That man, the one in the suit."

"I see him."

The boats drew closer. Blair could hear their roar as they bounced over the rough water.

The lone man kept his distance. He was short, bald, heavy-set. He could be an insurance agent, a teacher, a banker.

Or one of the men here to kill Michael.

The engine noise dropped to a rumble as both boats pulled up to shore. The Marine Patrol officers threw in lines, which the deputies caught. They pulled the boats up as close as they could, but everyone still had to wade up to their thighs to get in.

One boat, fully loaded, roared away. When Michael hung back, Blair waited, aware that he was watching the single man. She heard the slap of the waves against the remaining boat, felt the damp in the crisp breeze.

"Come on, Blair!" Evan shouted, drawing her attention. "Let's go!"

The stranger waded out to the boat. Michael, his hand warm and strong, led her out toward the small ladder at the rear of the boat. The choppy bay water pulled at Blair's clothing. Once on board, her wet clothes made her shiver. Michael pulled her against him as they sat on the deck.

"Your side," she said, pulling away.

"Will be better if you keep me warm." He didn't look at her; his attention remained fixed on the single man.

They settled back against the boat, braced for the bumpy ride. The trip across the bay took only minutes.

"Kevin!" Evan shouted when they neared land. "Keep an eye on the depth for me. I want to get as close as possible without running aground."

"Sure thing." Michael stood, his hand on Blair's shoulder.

She rose to her knees and peeked over the side. They

were coming into Osprey Landing, on the mainland. The pier had been ripped apart and lay in large pieces, bobbing on the water. Bay grass had caught smaller pieces of debris, holding it captive as it swayed with the movement of the water. It looked like a wasteland of lumber and driftwood. She glanced back toward Michael, and saw him peer into the water while the boat moved forward. Then he straightened and turned toward land.

She looked down at the water, so deep and dark. They were still out too far to walk to shore. The boat would have to pull in further to make it possible for everyone to get out. Blair looked toward land again, wondering where they planned to tie the boat. When she turned back toward Michael, a flash of movement caught her eye. Something shiny, probably some debris, had caught sunlight and reflected it from the thick pine woods to the left of the pier.

Michael disappeared overboard before she heard the sharp report of a gun shot.

Blair jumped up and ran toward the stern of the boat. The other passengers scrambled to the deck. The sound of a second shot filled the air as she reached the spot where Michael had stood.

"Get down!" Evan yelled.

She felt their forward motion stop, heard Evan shout again. Frantic, Blair watched the bobbing debris and sought the place where Michael must have gone under. Where he'd be.

Without thinking, she jumped in, felt the cool rush of water, the rough touch of broken wood. Breaking to the surface, she looked for Michael. For any sign. Then she began swimming the way they'd come. Grass swiped at her clothes and debris bumped her arms.

But he wasn't anywhere. There was nothing other

than wind and waves and debris.

She heard the boat coming toward her, slowly. Treading water, she looked in every direction. "Michael!" The wind threw his name back to her. Behind her, the boat engine idled.

A quick glance told her that the Marine Patrol officer who hadn't piloted the boat had jumped in.

"Blair!" Evan's voice came over the slap of the waves against the boat. "I've called for help."

The Marine patrol officer swam toward her and insisted she put on a life vest. What seemed like hours later, when the other Marine Patrol boat joined them, Blair thanked heaven for the officer's insistence as she struggled with arms that seemed more like lead weights.

Then Evan was there, treading water beside her.

Wiping his face, he said, "It's been too long. I'm sorry, Blair. You need to get out."

Chapter Four

Several hours later, the late morning breeze whipped around them as the boat bobbed up and down on the choppy bay. Blair, numb with disbelief, swaying with the motion of the boat, could see a milling crowd on shore.

The curious. Wanting to find out what had happened. Wanting to see the Marine Patrol and the Rescue Squad bring up Michael's body.

On the boat with Blair, Evan, and two Marine Patrol officers, stood the stranger who'd joined them for the ride across the bay. He'd introduced himself as Special Agent Abbott of the FBI. He'd even flipped open a badge for Evan and her to see. But all she could see was the cold in the man's eyes.

"What did you say Kevin's last name is?" Evan asked.

Unable to process anything, Blair barely heard the question. Only Evan's insistent look made her concentrate. "Kevin Johnson." She didn't question the lie. Bone deep cold made her pull the blanket Evan had given her tighter around herself.

"Blair," Evan's voice intruded. "I'm sorry, but we need his address, next of kin."

No time to think, to consider the consequences. "He's from Atlanta." Somehow, she managed to make up a street address when Evan persisted. The words came from the secret place she'd kept Michael for all these years. From the need to protect him.

When it was too late.

She looked at the floating storm debris, at the grass, waving in the crisp breeze.

Nothing. There had been no sign of him. Nothing in the hours since he'd fallen overboard.

"Family?"

Blair remembered the little she knew of Michael's family. His Argentinean father, an engineer, his American mother, his brother and sisters. "None. At least, not that I know of."

Special Agent Abbott said nothing. Why hadn't he identified himself earlier? He should have at least told Evan who he was.

Evan touched her arm. "I've arranged for you to go to my house. Becky'll be glad for the company."

"I need to go home." Get away from here. Run.

Forget.

"You shouldn't be alone now." Evan's eyes reflected a mixture of sadness and unease. A friend caught between genuine sympathy and the fear of a hysterical woman. But she'd given up the right to hysterics with a simple no.

"How long have you known Kevin?" Abbott's question cut through the silence.

"A few months." The lies were coming too quickly. She'd slip up soon, if she wasn't careful.

"Where did you meet?"

"In Atlanta." Abbott's silence made Blair clutch for something further to say. "I was there visiting friends."

"Where did he work?"

"He's a waiter."

"A waiter?" Abbott's brows shot up.

"At an Italian restaurant in Buckhead. I can't remember the name." Blair felt the boat engine rev, relieved to know she'd soon be away and not have to keep making up lies. She wasn't any good at it. There had to be a trap in something—everything—she'd said. Abbott would catch on.

Once on shore, Evan escorted her to a waiting Sheriff's Department cruiser and helped her in.

"Bob, take Ms. Davenport to my house. Becky's there."

"Sure thing, Evan," the deputy replied.

"Then drive over to Ms. Davenport's place and see how it did."

Before Evan could close the door, Abbott, who'd followed them, bent down toward Blair. "Here's my number, Ms. Davenport. If you think of anything that can help us notify Kevin Johnson's co-workers or family, please call me." He handed her a scrap of paper with a phone number penned on it.

Evan shut the door and Blair huddled down for the ride to his house. Thankfully, the deputy driving the cruiser didn't say anything. They drove through the storm ravaged bay front streets of the small town of Emerald Bay. Big live oaks and most power lines had fallen, but already crews were out clearing the streets, making way for power company trucks sent to restore electricity to the five thousand or so area residents. A few boats lay on their sides along the shore.

Evan's house, a single story brick ranch, sat in a quiet middle-class residential area of town. Blair's two-bedroom house was only a few blocks away. Becky, Evan's wife, had been a friend since Blair first began visiting her grandmother as a girl.

"Here we are, Ms. Davenport," the deputy said, pulling up in the drive.

Becky, dressed in shorts and T-shirt, blond hair pulled back in a ponytail, rushed out, leaving her front door wide open. She hugged Blair, blanket and all, as she got out of the cruiser.

"Oh, Blair! One of the deputies came by to tell me you'd gotten trapped on the island with Evan. How awful for you. Come on, let's get you inside. You can get a nice hot shower. We don't have power but we do have water and a gas water heater, so that's not a problem." Blair felt Becky's arm around her shoulder as Becky leaned down to talk to the deputy. "Thanks, Bob."

"Be back in a minute to let you know how your house looks," the deputy said after getting Blair's address.

Keeping up a non-stop barrage of conversation, none of which Blair responded to, Becky led her into the bathroom and took the now wet blanket. "Towels are here," she said, indicating a rack. "I've got some shorts you can wear and a top that should fit." She turned on the shower. "You go ahead. I'll leave the clothes in the spare room. Take your time."

Blair stripped and stepped into the shower, needing the warmth of the hot water. But she couldn't get warm.

She shouldn't feel Michael's absence so deeply. He hadn't been in her life in a long time, but she had always known he was somewhere.

How could he not be?

She blinked away tears and turned off the water, knocking the shampoo bottle down. She couldn't cry. Wouldn't.

"You okay?" Becky's question followed a knock on the bathroom door.

With determination born of the fear of feeling, Blair fumbled with the towel. "I'm fine!"

Once dressed, her hair towel-dried, she joined Becky in the living room. The curtains billowed in the damp breeze, the windows open to allow some circulation until the power was restored.

"You can stay as long as you like, Blair."

"I have to get back to my house and check on my classroom. I'll have to see about Grandma's house." She had to stay busy.

"Bob said you don't have any downed trees and the roof's okay." Becky patted her hand. "Don't worry about the school. That's what they pay principals for. As far as your grandmother's house, Evan dropped by before you got out of the shower. He said nobody's going to be allowed on the island until they're sure everything's safe."

Blair stared out the front window and watched the breeze whip the weeping willow in Becky's front yard. She had to find something to do, something to keep her focused, keep her mind off Michael. She couldn't let herself fall into a dark hole of grief.

"What happened, Blair?" Becky's softly worded question intruded on Blair's thoughts.

"What?" Blair's skin tingled at the unbidden memory of Michael calling himself Kevin. He'd been so calm about it. So casual, as if he pretended to be someone else all the time.

Because that was his job. His life.

"Evan said you were engaged to a Kevin Johnson."

How had Michael lived a life of lies? How had he hidden his true feelings? How had she? How would she?

Blair forced words out of her mouth. "Have they found him?"

Becky scooted closer to her on the couch. "No, sweetie. I'm sorry."

Blair looked outside again, at the tree, and hugged herself. Michael's beautiful body on the bottom of the bay was too horrible to think about.

Into the silence, Becky asked quietly, "Why didn't

you tell me about him?"

"I can't talk about it, okay?"

Becky nodded, but Blair saw beyond her friend's curiosity. Becky hesitated, then leaned closer to Blair. "Honey, I'm worried about you. Evan doesn't think there's anybody named Kevin Johnson. He says you were with Michael Alvarez."

"That's crazy!" But she knew her answer was too loud, too insistent.

"It's okay, Blair. I know you're upset." Becky took Blair's hands. "But when Evan described this Kevin, it sounded so much like Michael, I wondered, too. I know you haven't seen him—"

"Where did Evan get the idea that he's Michael?"

"From the FBI agent."

"Abbott?"

"I think that's what Evan said his name is."

Had Abbott set Michael up to be shot? That was crazy. Evan, not Abbott, had asked Michael to move forward on the boat.

"Evan says they're searching the edge of the bay. They'll continue to drag the bottom out by the landing until tonight."

Blair couldn't think about that. She concentrated on the willow in the breeze. But all she could picture was Michael's face. His dark eyes, his smile.

The shrill ring of the phone made Blair jump. Becky stood and answered, speaking quietly. Blair stared out the window, her mind numb.

"That was Evan. He says Drew's coming to town."

* * *

After spending most of the afternoon raking Becky's yard in a desperate attempt to forget, Blair borrowed Becky's car and drove to the landing. As wind whipped around her, she could see Saint's Island, now off limits to the mainland, across the dark bay waters.

"Did Abbott give you a business card?" Evan's voice broke into the solitude.

Blair turned toward him, surprised to see him. His cruiser was parked in the landing's lot. "No, he gave me a piece of paper with his phone number."

"No card?"

"No." She saw a frown on Evan's face. "What is it?"

"Have you called him?"

"I have nothing more to add."

Evan, his blue eyes worried, studied her. "Are you sure?"

"They've given up, haven't they?"

"I'm sorry, Blair. They had to go look for some other people, but they're pretty sure." He watched her carefully before continuing. "Current was strong because the tide was going out." Looking away, he pointed to a log floating on the choppy water. "See that? Well, this morning, that log would have floated to the island."

Blair watched the log and tried to stop thoughts of Michael's body floating on the bay.

"Is Kevin Johnson actually Michael Alvarez?" Evan's question blew around them.

"That's what I want to know, Blair."

Startled, Blair turned.

Drew stood a few feet behind Evan, looking tired and haggard, his brown hair tumbling onto his forehead.

Blair took in the hard light of his eyes. Beside her, Evan shifted.

"Is he?" Drew's insistent question cut across the sound of the breeze whipping the remains of the pier.

Blair couldn't gather enough breath to answer.

"Is Special Agent Abbott real?" Evan asked Drew, hands on his hips.

Drew looked from Blair to Evan. "Who?"

"Guy was on the island. Came across with us. Said he's FBI, investigating Alvarez. He flashed a badge. He's vanished now."

"What did he look like?"

Evan described him with a police officer's attention to detail.

"I'm in charge of the Alvarez investigation. No one named Abbott or fitting that description is with me."

Blair felt shivers on her arms. Abbott had to be Eddie. Michael had said he didn't know if Eddie was a good guy or a bad. The FBI were the good guys.

Drew hadn't hugged her. That, and the fact that he acted like a stranger, not her brother, stopped Blair from asking the questions that had plagued her from the moment Michael had asked her not to tell Drew that he was at Grandma Alice's.

"We have to find Michael." Drew's voice had a harshness Blair had never noted before.

"Marine Patrol had to call off the search," Evan said.

"Why were you after him?" Blair asked.

Drew looked pointedly at her. "He's in trouble, Blair. Big trouble. The kind that will get him killed."

It took a second for Blair to realize what Drew had said. "You believe he's alive?"

"The report I have says that a Kevin Johnson is presumed dead," Evan said.

Drew turned toward Evan. "Describe Johnson."

Again, Evan gave an accurate description.

"You met Michael." Accusation colored Drew's words as he turned toward Blair.

"Yes, I met him," Blair defended. "But only briefly, until that summer I was home. When you and Mitzi—"

"How well did you know him?"

"Well enough to know that whatever trouble he

might be in, he did nothing wrong."

Drew didn't reply. For long moments he stared at her as if deep in thought, then he turned away. Evan ducked his head, moving his hat from one hand to the other.

Finally, Drew turned back. "Hell, Blair." With that, he reached for his cell phone and punched in some numbers. Short moments later he put it away. "I can't get through. There's no signal." He looked at Evan. "Can you help me get in touch with my office?"

"I can try," Evan said, turning. "Come on and we'll give it a shot. It's not just the cell towers. Lines are still down all over the place. We can go to my house. For some weird reason, the phone there works." He walked toward his parked cruiser.

"Blair?" Drew hung back, his gaze directed across the bay. "Was Michael here as Kevin Johnson?"

Her answer came from grief, confusion, distrust. "No."

Drew's eyes narrowed. He bowed his head. Blair saw him take a deep breath before he looked up again. "When did you fall in love with him?"

The words to answer him wouldn't form. She shook her head.

"Damn, Blair."

"It had nothing to do with you," Blair said defensively.

"Maybe not then, but it does now."

* * *

Sleep eluded her. Blair tossed and turned in Becky and Evan's guest room. Power had not been restored and the air felt damp, the bed linen limp.

She'd wanted to go home, to hide herself away in her own house, but Becky had insisted. And when they'd gathered around a candle in the living room, listening to

Evan recount the amazing details of his day, laughing at the picture he painted of their pompous mayor, his Mercedes wrecked by a fallen limb, Blair had been thankful for the company.

But once alone, she couldn't blot out Drew's words, couldn't stop the memories from rolling over her. Finally, she gave in, sat up, propped on several pillows, and stared into the darkened night, her thoughts on the man who'd changed her life with a few simple words.

* * *

Six years earlier

"I'm Michael. Remember me?"

Blair looked up from the margarita she'd just been handed. The surprise of looking into smiling, intense brown eyes made her slosh the liquid on her hand. "Hi."

"I'm Drew's friend," he explained. One side of his mouth kicked up in a half smile, dark lashes accented the twinkle in his eyes.

Of course she remembered him. Who could forget? They'd bumped into each other for over a year, whenever he came home with Drew. Blair had always been on her way somewhere and only had a few moments to talk to him. Except for once, when he'd arrived in time for dinner. Afterwards, she'd been sure he had shown an interest, but the way he avoided her later, she was convinced she'd misread him.

"He's over there," Michael said, glancing toward where her brother stood talking to Mitzi Aldrich, the hostess of the party.

Blair nodded, unable to utter a word. This attitude was a complete about-face. She'd chalked up his silence during that one dinner to Drew's analysis of Michael's character as being one of the most dedicated new agents at his station, ex-military, not interested in anything beyond the job at hand. The man standing before Blair looked intent on picking her up.

"He won't mind if you interrupt," Blair managed, aware that Michael's eyes were on her bare shoulders. She'd chosen a spaghetti-strapped sun dress for the party because the early summer weather was too muggy for anything else. She stopped herself from touching the bodice.

"I don't know about that," he said. She hadn't noticed the rich timbre of his voice before.

The slow rhythm of a recent pop hit filled the air. Blair tried to back away, aware of the power of Michael's perusal. Around them, couples flowed together into the gentle beat and began dancing.

"Dance with me?" He held his hands out to her. Strong, long-fingered hands, with a sprinkling of dark hair on the tops. Blair's eyes followed up the length of his arms beyond the white cotton of his shirt, to the strong line of his throat, to his jaw. To the incredible dark eyes.

She moved toward him despite a momentary caution born of some silent instinct. He smelled so good. Clean, with a spicy aftershave. He felt so good. Strong, gentle, not trying to bring her any closer than her own comfort zone. If he knew how he'd destroyed the barriers of that zone with a single look, he'd pull her into the darkness of the night and—

"Are you here alone?" Michael's question rumbled across her senses.

"I came with Becky Landers." Out of the corner of her eye, Blair saw Becky, watching them.

"You have incredible shoulders."

They bumped into another dancing couple. Blair pulled away slightly and looked up at him. He was looking at her shoulders. A shoulder man? She laughed.

He stopped dancing and held her at arm's length. His smile, so far removed from the self-confidence he'd radiated only moments before, made Blair stare. She could almost see a flush across his strong cheekbones. "I usually do better when I make a pass."

"Was that a pass?"

"I think it was meant to be." He held her with his eyes. "But it's the truth."

She felt off balance. There was truth there. And something else. Something she'd never seen before. Something beyond the simple fact that Michael wasn't treating her with kid gloves, the way he had before, the way other men treated her. Like a Davenport. She stepped toward him again, effortlessly fitting against him as they picked up the rhythm.

"Drew says you're a senior at Hollins College."

Blair wanted to deny attendance at the elite college. She wanted to be someone else for a man she thought would care little about such things. But she was who she was. "Yes."

"Near Roanoke, right?"

"Yes."

"That's home?"

"Mmhm." She felt boneless, felt the movement of his body against hers. A picture of them, his dark head next to hers brought a heat to her cheeks. She pulled away.

"Okay?"

She cleared her throat. She couldn't seem to control her reactions. Whatever poise she'd learned from dealing with the social life she'd been born to, fled the moment Michael Alvarez took her in his arms. "Yes."

He pulled her against him again, this time closer. This time she went beyond her comfort zone and felt the warmth of his hand trace a line down her back to her waist. Blair pushed aside the caution she'd felt moments ago and flowed into Michael's rhythm, closing her eyes against a dark foreboding lingering on the periphery of her consciousness.

* * *

Hours later, music wafted across the moonlit patio. Michael held her close, moving to the rhythm of the music. The party had spilled outside. Now a small group of couples danced in the warm night breeze.

"What would Drew say if he saw us?"

Blair laughed. "Drew left hours ago. With Mitzi."

"She's the hostess, isn't she?"

"Mmhm." She didn't want to talk about Drew, about anything.

"What would he say?"

Blair drew back. The moonlight that glanced off Michael's strong features gave a blue sheen to his black hair. "Does it matter?"

"For what I have in mind, yes." His words sent hot shivers up her arms.

Her breath caught in her throat. "What do you have in mind?"

"This." Blair saw him bend toward her, blocking the light with the beauty of his face, and felt the hot, soothing touch of his mouth on hers.

Blair had never been seduced by a kiss. Michael's mouth coaxed her into want. Gentle pressure, the hot seal of hungry lips, the tantalizing pressure of hands holding her tight, all combined to spark desire.

And she gave in to it. Passion slid new, sparkling and alive, into her consciousness. When Michael pulled away, moonlight glistened on his lips, still parted. Drawn to touch, to feel, Blair reached up and rubbed shaky fingers across his lower lip. In the half-light of the patio, she saw his tongue touch her fingers, felt heaviness well in her stomach. She gasped and looked into his eyes, so hot, so full of wonder.

He bent to her again, taking her mouth in an erotic kiss that couldn't end—didn't end. The textures, the scents, the very essence of Michael Alvarez came to her in that single instant.

And she knew she was lost.

* * *

The present

Blair woke with a sob, trying to keep from crying out. She'd fallen asleep in Becky's guest room, remembering. Her dream, which started out so sweetly, had become a nightmare when Michael jerked out of her arms, fell back and looked down at himself. Red had bloomed on his left side; confusion etched his face as he looked behind her. Blair had turned to see what he saw.

The dark shadow of a man stood at the edge of the patio, a smoking gun in his hand.

She held her hand over her mouth to stop the scream of horror buried beneath the knowledge that she'd betrayed Michael.

Because the man with the gun was Drew."

Chapter Five

Blair's house had survived Nell, but it took her, with Becky's help, all the next morning to rake up the storm debris in her yard. Afterwards, she'd asked Becky to take her to a car rental place. Now in her rental, she went back to Osprey Landing and walked around, hoping she'd find footprints, something, that would tell her Michael had made it to shore.

Because Drew seemed sure Michael was alive.

Because her dream had been so vivid.

But there were too many footprints. The Sheriff's Department, the Marine Patrol and the Rescue Squad had all combed the landing. Besides, she had no way of recognizing Michael's footprints among all of those.

She looked across the mile-and-a-half stretch of water, trying to figure out what to do. Inactivity would bring the memories back. Fidgety, too wired up to relax, she dreaded the thought of going back home.

If she could stay busy, maybe get to school and check on her classroom, she wouldn't drive herself crazy. Going to Grandma's was impossible. She'd checked with the authorities and she would not be allowed across. The Marine Patrol had been ordered to arrest anyone attempting to get to the island. Power lines were down, they said. It was a big, dangerous mess.

Wind pushed at her hair, pulled at her shirt and sent choppy waves crashing at her feet. Someone had disregarded orders and had a sleek, colorful catamaran skipping across the water. As it rushed toward her, she caught sight of the man struggling to keep the cat upright in the strong wind. What an idiotic thing to do.

She found she'd walked back nearly to the pier. In the parking lot, she saw Evan and one of the Marine Patrol officers who'd brought them over from the island the day before. They talked intently, then Evan pointed toward the bay.

Blair turned and saw a Marine Patrol boat cutting across the water, spraying foam as it roared toward Saint's Island.

"What's going on?" Blair shouted, hurrying toward them.

When she reached Evan and the officer, Evan said, "Drew's on his way to the island with a search crew."

"But I was told it's too dangerous to go over."

"It is for the residents."

"Why is Drew going?"

Evan shook his head and shrugged. "He's FBI. He can do whatever he wants."

* * *

Blair drove away from Osprey Landing after refusing Evan's invitation to stay with them for a few days. Blair assured him she was fine. But she wasn't. Sanity lay in taking charge, so she drove toward the one place that had given her a sense of fulfillment.

Felled trees lay in pieces beside the road and, up ahead, power company trucks were lowering their ladders. A moment later, Emerald Bay Elementary came into view, and Blair saw lights inside. Power had been restored. As she pulled up in front of the modern brick schoolhouse, she saw a number of cars, all belonging to other teachers. The principal's car was parked in its usual spot.

Under the afternoon sun, Blair searched the shady

outside of the building for damage. It was only as she stepped out of her car that she saw it.

Two huge oaks had crashed onto the west wing of the school. Her wing. Slamming the car door, she ran toward the side of the building. Ellen Thompson, a first grade teacher whose room was next to hers, stood like a statue, staring at the rubble that had once been her classroom.

"Ellen?"

Ellen turned, her face pale and devoid of expression. "It's gone, Blair. Nell took all of it. There's nothing left."

Mr. Adams, the principal, came from the side door of the building, dressed in shorts and a T-shirt. Blair had never seen him dressed so informally, but then, nothing like Nell had ever befallen them.

"Blair," he called. "You've got some damage."

Blair felt her heart tighten.

"Your classroom's not as bad as Ellen's. I'm taking her home. There's nothing she can do here. Bill Smith's in your room, if you want to check things out. Fire department said we can go in."

Blair hurried toward the building, then turned from the door to see Mr. Adams take Ellen by the arm. Poor Ellen. She'd been teaching for twenty years. She had no family. Nell had destroyed her world.

Bill, the art teacher who looked more like a basketball coach, was straightening some of the desks in her room. "It could have been a lot worse, Blair," he said.

With a quick look around, she agreed. One of the windows she'd boarded up had been crushed by one of the trees. Rain and wind had come in, but over-all, it wasn't bad. She'd have to throw away a lot of the extra material she'd collected. It would take her a few days to get everything back the way she wanted it once the repairs were done.

"How's your classroom?" she asked.

"Fine. It's only the two trees that landed on this side of the building that did any damage." He straightened another desk. "Looks like you got some rain damage, but if we pull everything over to this side, you should be okay. The wind blew some stuff around, too."

"I can take care of it, Bill, thanks." She didn't want to encourage Bill's attention. Tall, blond and handsome, Bill had asked her out a few times, showing much more interest in her than she showed in him.

"You sure?"

"I've got nothing better to do."

Bill left moments later, leaving Blair to reflect on her last words to him.

Nothing better. She'd never said that about her work. Another few years and she'd be like Ellen Thompson, with no life beyond school.

No. She was more than just a teacher, or a woman dependent first on her family and name, or dependent on a job, as much as she might love it. But what if she'd yes to Michael?

She'd be in mourning.

She refused to let that word sink in, so she focused on her classroom. Amid the scattered papers, she found a painting one of her students had done. The bright red catamaran the child had painted floated on too blue water. It was now marred by four drops of rain. The curve of white sand against impossibly green grass reminded her of the catamaran she'd seen earlier.

And of the cat she'd sailed with Michael six years earlier. His powerful body guiding the craft across the bay to a cove on Saint's Island.

Michael, who swam strong and sure, sleek as a

dolphin.

A vague idea nudged her mind, then took hold.

Could an injured, strong swimmer go that distance if he held on to debris?

Struggling to stop herself from rushing out, she looked around the room that represented everything to which she'd devoted herself. Things were in disarray, but the really important elements weren't here anyway: the small sticky hands, the lopsided smiles, the quick laughter. She would have those back when school started again in a few weeks. Everything would be in order by then, she'd make sure of that.

But right now, the pull of what could be, pushed her out the door and to her car.

* * *

Within the light of pre-dawn, Blair heard the soft lapping of waves along the bay shore. Thank heaven it was a calm morning, because it would be a long one.

Blair had borrowed a canoe from her neighbor, an older man who'd evacuated but had left it trailered to the small pickup he owned. She'd called him and asked if she could use it for trip down Cold Water Creek, an area further north, unaffected by Nell. She'd thanked him, probably too profusely, and taken the paddles and life vest he'd offered.

Getting the canoe into the water by herself had not been fun, and hiding even such a small truck with its attached trailer in the trees had proven challenging, especially in the dark. Finally, she grabbed her shoes and backpack, and placed them on the back seat of the canoe before climbing in.

She should be asleep now, resting so she could reclaim her room from the storm damage. Instead, she'd lost her mind. Over Michael again. Over a wild, unrealistic hope that Drew knew something.

Pushing off, she paddled steadily, the sun casting its first light across the bay. Luckily, the tide was with her, carrying her toward Saint's Island. Luckier still, no barges or Marine Patrol boats were on the water. Even so, it took longer than she'd expected to get across.

The golden ball of early morning sun cleared the horizon as she eased in to a tiny cove where vines tumbled right down to the water. She hurried to pull the canoe up on shore into a thicket of scrub oak. Her legs shook, her arms felt like rubber. Heaven knew how long it would take to walk to Grandma's. She'd had no sleep to speak of in forever. Looking toward the rough terrain of the island, she made up her mind. She had to rest. She stepped back into the canoe and curled up, using the backpack as a pillow.

* * *

Men's voices intruded on Blair's consciousness, as did bright light and droning bugs.

Startled, she roused herself from light sleep, remembering where she was and why.

She listened intently, not daring to move a muscle.

The voices faded in and out, caught on the morning breeze. It had to be Drew and his search crew. No one was allowed on Saint's Island. They'd either spent the night searching or had come back this morning. Hoping she couldn't be seen because of the scrub oaks, she grabbed her backpack, climbed out of the canoe, and covered it with vines, grass and any debris she could find.

Crouched low, she hid behind a large clump of gnarled scrub oaks and flattened herself on the sand. She listened as the men drew nearer.

"He's not here, Drew."

"He has to be," her brother replied.

"He's probably dead. He took a bullet."

"If anybody could survive, it's Michael."

"I know he's a friend, Drew, but you're giving him too much credit. He wasn't at your grandmother's house. We spent all of yesterday afternoon and this morning looking for him. If he is here, we're not going to find him unless we go door-to-door. There aren't enough of us."

Drew didn't reply for a long time, then finally said, "Damn it."

"What do we do?"

"We head back and arrange for more men."

* * *

Blair's shirt stuck to her back. Perspiration trickled down her temple. She'd never walked from the bay side of the island all the way to Grandma's. Walking it now, with the tangle of hurricane debris, was hard. The backpack she carried, full of first aid supplies, clean clothes and water, weighed more with each step she took. The sight of Alpert's Lake, its dark waters rippling in the breeze, made her pause.

Island lore said there was an alligator.

She was so alone. Drew and his men had left—she'd watched their boat speed across the bay. She had no way to communicate with anyone. Her cell phone had been useless, so she'd left it at home.

She didn't really believe there was an alligator. After all, Grandma Alice had shown her an article in the paper that said wildlife officials had not found one. But as late morning gave way to noon and shortening shadows created bright, shimmering shapes on the waters of the lake, Blair found she wasn't as brave as she had thought she was. She stopped to rest twice on her way around the lake, splashing the tannin-stained water on her face and neck to fight off the sticky heat.

When she jumped at the sound of a frog hitting the

water, she laughed at herself. She'd taken leave of her senses, broken official orders by disregarding warnings to stay away from the island, gambling on the remote possibility that Michael was alive, yet a frog had made her jump out of her skin.

As she rounded what she hoped was the last curve in the lake before she could strike out for the house, she prayed that she was right, that Michael had come back here.

If he hadn't, this would be it. She wouldn't—couldn't—invest any more of her tangled emotions in Michael.

If he was alive.

Alpert's Lake sometimes broke out into the Gulf and the closer she got to the Gulf, the more debris floated on the lake. Not only vegetation but pieces of housing insulation and plastic of one kind or another. A shampoo bottle bobbed on the tiny breaking waves.

Movement caught her eye. The dark waters moved in the bright light, ripples traveling to each shore.

Blair's breath caught.

The alligator.

She shaded her eyes and squinted. As the alligator rose from the water, she grabbed the shampoo bottle, prepared to throw it and run.

"What the hell are you doing here, Blair?"

It wasn't an alligator.

Michael stood waist deep in Alpert's Lake, his wet hair dripping into his eyes, and cursed his lack of attention. If he'd been as careless when Drew had been here, he'd be dead now. He spoke into the heat of midday. "Are you going to shoot me with a shampoo bottle?"

"Are you out of your mind? Half the country is looking for you and you're standing there naked?"

The crack in her voice told him how badly he'd frightened her. "I don't have spare clothes I can afford to bathe in."

The arm that held the shampoo bottle dropped to her side. "Drew is looking for you."

"So what the hell are you doing here?"

"I think I was under some misguided notion that you might be hurt. Or dead."

"You should have stayed away, Blair."

"And wonder for the rest of my life if you're on the bottom of the bay?"

"It takes more than a bad shot to finish me off."

"Maybe a shot like the one you took in your side?"

She had a point, of course. Blair could dish it out. He hadn't seen that before. "You didn't think breaking the law by coming on the island would attract attention?" Michael stepped as close to her as he dared, careful to keep his lower body under water.

"No one saw me," she said defensively, her back straight, her eyes angry. "How are you going to get off?"

"Unless I can find a boat, the only possible way." He wiped a hand down his face. "Swim."

"You can't swim back." The flashing anger in her eyes gave way to something deeper, more meaningful. "You're not strong enough."

He bit back his instant response that he'd gotten here just fine by swimming because it wasn't fair. She'd come to help. Having her care touched emotions he didn't want to deal with. "Turn around or close your eyes." He hoped she'd interpret the hoarseness of his voice as reaction to exhaustion.

For a single moment, he thought she'd do neither, then he saw her straighten and turn away, her concentration on the horizon.

He got out of the water as quickly as possible, dried

off with his shirt and struggled, still damp, into his dirty, clammy clothes.

"Drew was on the island."

"I know." He reached out to touch her shoulder. "Have you talked to him?"

She turned, her eyes searching his. "Yesterday. He believes you're alive."

"Did you tell him I was with you?"

"No." She shook her head. "But he didn't believe me."

She wasn't a good liar. He was. He couldn't let her see his suspicions of Drew. And, he admitted, he couldn't face the knowledge that she would believe Drew. "Did he explain why he's after me?"

"It's not just him, Michael, it's other people, too, but you know that. Why don't you explain it to me?"

"It's too complicated."

"I'm pretty smart. I even have a college degree now."

Sarcasm wasn't something she'd ever used before, another surprise. "You're Drew's sister."

She blinked, her green eyes clouded with confusion. Then she took a short breath. "You don't trust him."

"Stay out of it, Blair."

"I'm in it already. He's my brother. I deserve to know."

"He told you about me when you asked?" He saw the flush of anger color her cheeks. "I didn't think so."

"He's doing his job."

"Did you tell him you deserve to know about me?"

She met his gaze squarely. "If the question is whether or not he knows about us from before, he does."

"Hell."

"Did you expect me to show no emotion when I thought you were dead?"

"That I might die didn't make any difference to you

six years ago." He wanted to call the words back the moment he said them.

Blair's breath left her body. Of course it mattered. She fought to keep tears from forming.

"Blair, I'm—" Michael took a step closer to her, so close she could see the tiny scar on his upper lip. She felt the brush of his hand along her cheek.

"I shouldn't have said that. I'm sorry, Blair. You have nothing to feel bad about."

But she did. She'd missed all those years. She'd slammed the door on a future. And she'd done it out of fear. She was still afraid, but now it was different. The fear was a real menace, not a girl's fear of losing a simple dream of happily ever after. Not as simple as being afraid of wanting what she knew she couldn't handle, couldn't keep.

"Please, let's not talk about what happened." Her voice sounded ragged, even to herself.

"Can we put the past behind us?"

She couldn't. Just the sound of the question, asked so softly, did funny things to her. Made her remember the feel of him, so gentle, so wild. She felt her cheeks burn, felt the crush of all she'd said no to.

"We can't, can we?" He cupped her chin and tilted her face up toward his. "But remembering doesn't change how it was. Nothing can change that."

How it was? She wanted to yell at him. She hadn't been strong enough or brave enough to give up her dreams to be with him, but he didn't give them a chance by refusing to really talk to her.

Sanity and honesty prevailed. "No, nothing can change what happened. Not even your death."

"I don't plan on dying any time soon." He released her chin.

"That's why I'm here."

He raised an eyebrow.

"I have a boat. I came to get you off the island."

* * *

Blair Davenport still had the ability to surprise him. The first time Michael had seen her, he'd been attracted to her through what had to be a twenty-eight-year-old's biological response to a beautiful young woman. At least that's what he'd told himself as he managed to avoid her for over a year of accidental meetings. Then he'd seen the real Blair. The one she kept hidden. The one who'd surfaced the night he'd accompanied Drew to a party. A week before he was to be given the chance to avenge his brother's death.

To this day, he could remember the way she looked in the dress she'd worn, the thin straps across her incredible shoulders. He'd been caught staring. That was the last time he'd blushed, embarrassed at his thoughts of a friend's sister. They'd walked away from the party and gone to her grandmother's. The moon had been bright that night and they'd gone outside. He'd felt like a teenager, eager to sit with his arm around his girl.

They'd sat on the porch, talking for hours, and she'd revealed who she was beneath the outer trappings.

"Have you ever thought about traveling in space?" She'd looked up, her head tilted back, the line of her throat clean. "I've always wanted to," she said in a wistful tone.

Her words were so unexpected that his hand dropped to her bare shoulder. Then the feel of her skin stopped his thoughts. Struggling, he sat a little straighter. "You have?" Somehow, Blair Davenport, so blessed with beauty, charm and wealth, wanting to break free, surprised him.

"I wanted to fly jets," she'd laughed lightly. "Drew said I was crazy."

"What did your parents say?"

"Oh, I didn't tell them."

"Why not?"

She'd looked at him, the moon reflected in her eyes. "It's not something they would expect from me."

He wanted to ask what they did expect, but he knew. A good marriage to a successful member of their social set. She wouldn't get that from him.

But he knew what he could give her. "Want to come fly with me?"

* * *

Reality wasn't as wistful, or as easy, Michael acknowledged. They wouldn't fly to Alice's. They'd have to walk through palmetto and scrub oak, and wend their way through storm debris.

Blair looked at the narrow path. "Where did you hide while Drew was here?"

"In a garage on the bay side of the island." He reached for the backpack Blair had brought.

"I can carry it."

"Let me be a gentleman about something, Blair."

"You were always a gentleman."

That surprised him. He didn't think he'd been a gentleman at all. He'd been crazy with the need for her, with the need to feel after the loss of David. Blind to all the problems, the consequences of his actions. They'd both paid for his blindness.

He took the backpack. "Do you know what Drew intends to do?"

"I heard him this morning before he left. He's gone back to get more men to go door to door."

"He's convinced I'm here." Drew Davenport wouldn't give up. Michael should have seen that trait in his sister.

"We have to leave."

"How did you get here?"

"I borrowed a canoe."

Michael shook his head. She could have drowned.

"It's really sturdy. Both of us will fit nicely."

"When did you cross?"

She stopped and looked up at him. "Don't worry. Drew didn't see me. I came across just before light."

"Damn, it Blair!"

"He didn't see me! No one did!"

"That's not the point." He reached out with his free hand and grabbed her shoulder. "No one knew you were out there. Don't you know how dangerous that was?"

"I had a life vest and it was really calm."

He looked up at the sky, trying to control the fear that the vision of her on the lonely bay had brought to mind. He released his hold on her, turned, and began walking. Up above, a jet's trail arced across the blue sky.

It ripped six years of time from his grasp. Six years during which he'd tried to forget Blair. What he remembered told him what he should have known about her, about why she'd crossed the bay in a canoe.

The memory rushed at him as clearly as the green of her eyes had stayed with him.

* * *

Six years earlier

"Are you sure about this?" Blair shouted over the sound of the wind rushing past them as they drove Michael's Jeep, top off, down the highway.

"You'll love it."

He could already see the excitement in her eyes. She was cautious, though, not ready to give in to the thrill of it. But she would. He knew she would.

"Your friend will have time to take us up?"

"Doesn't matter," he said, "I'm taking us up."

He glanced at her, anxious to see her expression, afraid she might balk at the thought. But Blair laughed too, and with a quick glance at his hands on the steering wheel, she grabbed a handful of her hair to keep it from flying around her head.

Michael's second moment of doubt came when they pulled up at John's airfield. John didn't have grand ambitions and his airfield showed it. Michael was sure it was nothing like the private airfield the Davenports frequented. And John was nothing like any Davenport mechanic. A Columbian by birth, John was really named Juan, but claimed to be more American than any American. And probably was.

Dressed in greasy blue overalls, he came running when he spotted Michael. "*Hola*, Miguel!"

Michael got out of the car and shook John's hand. "*¿Qué tal*, Juan?"

"You bring a pretty lady to fly?"

Blair didn't give Michael time to come around to help her out of the car. He held his hand out to her as she walked around to his side. "Blair, this is John Rodriguez. John, Blair Davenport."

"It is a pleasure, Señorita."

To Michael's immense pleasure, Blair didn't hesitate to shake John's stained hand. "I hope we're not interrupting."

"No, no," John shook his head. "Michael, he can interrupt all the time. No, for Michael I will walk on hot coals, no Miguel?"

Afraid of where the conversation might stray, Michael decided to get on with it. "You have a plane I can borrow for an hour?"

John's eyes lit up. "Do I have a plane? *Claro*, yes." He turned and began walking toward a hanger. "Come,

come."

Moments later they stood beside a bright yellow bi-plane. Juan looked at Blair. "*Es hermosa ¿no?*"

"Very beautiful," Blair's voice surprised both men. She was looking at the plane with wonder.

Michael felt a rush of affection, of pride, at her obvious delight.

"You will enjoy, I know," John said. "Michael will take you where eagles fly." He laughed, looking at them both, as Michael wondered which part of his heart would stay with Blair after he left.

He and John pushed the plane out of the hanger and moments later they lifted off.

Blair Davenport was born to fly. Her thrill at the sights and feel of being aloft was palpable. Michael took them low over the beach, up and over gentle loops.

And Blair laughed for the joy of freedom, trusting completely in his ability.

* * *

The present

Back at Alice's, Michael washed his face using water Blair had stored in the bathtub and changed out of his damp, filthy clothes into some Drew had left behind. The shirt was too tight across the shoulders, and the shorts, a little loose, tended to slide down, but Michael didn't care. They were cleaner than what he'd been wearing after his lake bath. There would be no real baths here, only rinses that saved what water they did have, since without power, the electric well didn't work.

Both exhausted, Blair and he napped outside on old quilts, beneath scrub oak, close to Alice's, until sunset. If Drew came back, they'd hear him.

The house itself was too hot to stay inside even after dark, so they brought their meal out to the deck where moonlight spilled across the night. They'd warmed soup on a camp stove Blair had found in the storage room. Somehow, she'd also warmed some cold, hard rolls.

"Water or soda?" she asked, holding paper cups.

"Water's fine."

She opened one of several gallon jugs, part of every beach resident's hurricane kit. Michael told himself he'd have to remember to bury the trash or whoever came into the house next would know someone had been here after the storm.

With the outdoor furniture still stored, they sat cross-legged on the deck and ate.

"How's your shoulder? Your side?" Blair asked moments later.

"Sore, but much better. I think swimming did me some good."

"I doubt it." Her quick reply made him aware, again, of the differences between this Blair and the one he'd known. She'd changed from the woman who'd easily agreed to fly loops across the sky with him. "We can leave tomorrow."

"Leave tomorrow?" he repeated.

"I hid the truck and trailer, but I'd rather not leave them there too long. Someone could stumble on to them."

"Where did you hide them?"

She paused, the spoon halfway to her mouth. He couldn't see her eyes clearly, but he saw her face tilt upward toward him. "Sunrise Cove."

Michael felt his heart slam into his chest. He wouldn't remember Sunrise Cove. He couldn't. "Blair—"

"It seemed like a good place," she hurried to add. "It's in the trees."

He tried to swallow, tried to get beyond the

memories that rushed at him from every direction. The joy of their passion, the hurt of her refusal. He nodded, pushing desperately at the picture he'd conjured of Blair with her hair wild around her face, falling over them both.

"No one would think to look there." Her words barely registered on his inflamed senses.

Sunrise Cove. Michael wondered if her memories of that morning were as vivid as his. Or did she only remember the end of that morning and the last words he'd hurled at her as she'd left him and he'd gone on to the life that led him to this point in time?

"Why?" The question formed from the recesses of his thoughts. He never meant to voice it.

She put her spoon down carefully. "Please don't," she whispered.

"Don't?" He tried to tamp down the tension in his body. "Don't what, Blair? Don't remember what it was like? I haven't thought of anything else for six years. How it ended? I've cursed myself for a fool for six years over that."

"I couldn't do it, Michael," she whispered.

He remembered the cruelty of what he'd said, the passion of the man he'd been. At twenty-two, she had been young, too young in experience for him, but he'd wanted her.

He'd been a real bastard. "I never meant to hurt you."

She shook her head and swiped quickly at her cheek. "You were gentle." She paused for a second. "And kind. And fun."

Michael felt her words like a knife against his heart. All those things. But no trust. Not the one thing that could have bound them together.

He heard her take a deep breath, saw her bow her

head for a moment. Then she looked up at him, the softness of her lips visible in the pale light. "Let's not dredge it up. Please."

She was right. There was no point in remembering. They'd moved beyond the past, to the present.

She stood abruptly, taking the plates and utensils they'd used, and piled them together. "Drew won't stop until he finds you."

"I know."

"Whatever he thinks, he's wrong."

"Don't think too highly of me, Blair. I've done things that would make your hair stand on end."

"You don't want me to believe in you?"

"I want you to realize what I've had to do. The life I've lived. It's not pristine and safe and pretty."

The silence of night closed around them. "Has it changed you?"

He paused, wishing he could tell her, wishing suddenly, that he had before. If only he'd understood it then. "Everything that happens to us changes us. Haven't you changed?"

Blair heard the edges of some emotion in Michael's words, that emotion he had hidden from her before. She stood and walked toward the deck railing, her back to him. "Yes, I've changed."

Behind her she heard Michael stand, heard his bare feet against the deck as he walked toward her. The weight of his hand on her shoulder made her turn.

"We can't go back, Blair. There's no fixing the past." Against the backdrop of moonlight, he looked bigger, darker.

"No, we can't go back," she agreed. His words hurt. Nearly made her crumple. But if nothing else, she was a realist.

He had not forgiven her for refusing. There was no

future for them. While they might have both changed in some ways, in other, more basic ways they hadn't. He still didn't trust her enough to tell her his secrets and she still couldn't hope to keep up with the wild ride a life with him would entail.

The warm roughness of his hand on her cheek made her tilt her face to increase the pressure.

God, how she'd missed this. Him.

"Damn it, Blair," the words seemed dragged from him. "We've had nothing but lousy timing."

His face moved down toward her and she knew, just as she had so long ago.

Michael would break her heart.

His mouth found hers quickly, moved on hers softly, and pushed her to where only he had ever taken her.

To passion. To memories of what she'd felt with him. They overwhelmed her. Michael overwhelmed her.

Chapter Six

Six years earlier

He was kissing her, standing one step below her at Grandma Alice's, his mouth open and giving and hot. Drawing her into madness, into desire.

She ran her fingers through the dark strands of his hair, felt the pull of the kiss, so deep and wild. They'd just come back from the airfield and she felt like she was flying again, turning loops in John's airplane.

A sound intruded on her thoughts and she jumped, pulling away. Michael, too, jumped, and moved down another step.

"Blair?" Her grandmother's voice came from the open door above them.

"Yes, Grandma, it's me."

"Bring your young man in, dear. I've made lunch."

Blair looked down at Michael. His eyes still blazed with a heat rivaling that of the midday sun.

"Thank you, Mrs. Davenport, but I need to go take care of some things." He looked at Blair, making her heart turn a little somersault. "I'll pick you up at three?"

"Yes." She sounded as breathless as she'd felt when they turned the first loop.

Grandma Alice closed the door and went back inside.

Standing so close, Blair noticed a scar on Michael's upper lip, a tiny upside down "V" that formed a ridge.

Without thinking, she reached out a hand and touched it. "How did you get that?"

His gaze flew to hers and she saw a darkness there that she hadn't seen before. "My brother kicked a soccer ball into my face."

She tried to move her hand away, but the darkness passed and he pressed a kiss to the palm. Tingles ran all the way to her toes.

Michael grabbed her hand and pulled her down the steps to his car. "I have a friend who can lend me a catamaran," he said with a smile that made his eyes light up again. "Want to try it?"

"I've never done it. I don't know how." But he could have asked her to shoot for the moon and she would have gone with him.

"I know exactly what to do."

Suddenly she understood a deeper, more heart-stopping meaning in his words.

Come with me, he was saying. Come with me for what I can show you.

* * *

The present

She'd wanted him just as she did now, with no thought of yesterdays, tomorrows or consequences. Just Michael, here and now.

She let her hands drop from his arms to his hips, felt the inevitability of the kiss turn into hungry insistence. The texture, the taste of him, permeated her very soul. She'd missed too much, wanted him for too long to feel the least hesitation.

He broke the kiss, running his hands up her back, tunneling his fingers through her hair, holding her to him as his mouth trailed down her neck, pulling aside her blouse to kiss her shoulder. Tiny shocks of pleasure made her tremble, made her hungrier. She grappled with his T-shirt, tugging until he stepped back to allow her to pull the thing up and over his head. It fell to the deck and she stood on tiptoes to bury her face in his neck, to press heated kisses to resilient flesh.

She felt his fingers fumbling over her blouse buttons, trembled as he brushed against her breasts. Then he pushed the blouse open and stepped back. Instinctively, she moved to cover herself, aware that the flimsy lace of her bra hid nothing.

"No, don't," he said in a sandpaper voice. "You're so beautiful. I've dreamed about you for so long."

She let her hands drop to her sides. She let her blouse slip off her arms, terribly conscious of every breath. He ran his hands along the back of the bra.

"It fastens in the front," she whispered.

No turning back now. No wanting to turn back.

With the moonlight behind him, darkness and shadows all around, she couldn't read his face as he released the front catch of the bra.

Then he was there with gentle touches, softer kisses. A fevered mouth tugging at her, binding her to him as he had so long ago. But it was different now. Now there was urgency and knowledge.

He came back to her mouth, crushing her to him. The passion in his body felt so strong, so right. She leaned back against the railing and he followed, the weight of him joyous.

She felt his hands cup her behind, felt him raise her toward him, felt herself melt.

Then, suddenly, he turned away, running a shadowy hand roughly through his hair. The sea breeze sent a chill through her.

"Michael?" She heard a catch in her voice.

He stood a few feet away from her, his hands

gripping the railing next to him, his breathing rough and unsteady. Even in the dim light she could see the control he was trying to summon. Moments later, he straightened, the muscles in his back taut. His harsh laugh filled the night. "This can't happen."

Trying to convince herself that Michael's laugh had humor behind it, Blair replied, "I think it can."

"Damn it, Blair. We can't do this." He spoke the words into the stiff breeze.

Blair took a quick breath. "It felt doable to me," she said trying desperately to ward off the tears she knew would soon run unchecked down her cheeks.

He spun around, and in the play of shadows, she saw what she'd heard in his voice. Passion, pure and simple.

"Don't. It's taking everything I have not to drag you into the bedroom and satisfy every fantasy I've agonized over for six god awful years. Don't push me."

"I'm not denying you."

He moved back toward her quickly and gripped her shoulders. "I have no way to protect you, Blair."

And that brought reality crashing down. Brought the past right into the present. Made her remember the feel of the words he'd used when she refused to go with him. She tried to twist away.

He held her upper arms. "Don't, Blair. Listen. Listen and believe me when I tell you I'm sorry for everything. For what I said." He tried to gentle her with those words, with sweet pressure from magical hands gliding up to ease the tension in her shoulders, her neck. "I wanted to call you, to take the words back."

"Let go of me," she said, her heart thudding against her ribs. She couldn't replay their parting.

He released her. "I shouldn't have let you go then. I should have—"

"What?" She fought the wobble in her voice by

speaking louder. "Waited a few weeks to find out if I was pregnant?"

He released her then, his head bowed. "I don't know why you weren't. We never used—"

"I wouldn't have considered a pregnancy," she paused to take a shallow breath so she could continue and be sure he heard her choked repetition of the words he'd used, "the consequences of sleeping with the hired help."

A long silence preceded his next words. "It was a shameful thing to say, Blair. I was angry. Hurt. Stupid."

Just as she'd been. Just as she was now. Only now she was mature enough to give voice to what had bubbled inside her for six years. "We didn't know each other at all, did we? You really thought I was so shallow that I only wanted a good time."

"No, Blair. I didn't think at all." Regret laced his words. "Would you have told me if you were?"

This was where they were different. He was sorry for what he said. He would have done things differently. She could only be as honest. For an entire week after he left, she'd wondered the same thing. "I don't know."

He tensed and moved away from her. "You're right. We didn't know each other. It went too fast." With a single breath, he added, "We can't afford to gamble again."

* * *

Hours later Michael lay awake on the wide guest room bed. He'd opened the windows, hoping a breath of the cooler air that had finally come in behind Nell would stir the damp heat of the house, but it didn't help.

The heat came from inside him. From suppressed passion, from gut wrenching need. He'd stripped to his shorts, aware that short of taking Blair, his only recourse was a cool dip in the Gulf or the lake.

Rolling over, he punched the pillow, wincing at the painful pull of his injuries, trying to bury the hurt of Blair's honesty, to erase from his mind what should have been.

If he hadn't used those words when she'd said no. She wouldn't have said no if he'd been someone else. If he'd given her more. If she'd trusted him.

He wouldn't think about it now. He'd spent too long thinking about it. The man he'd been had ended their future years ago. Going back to replay the desperate emotions wouldn't change a damn thing.

They were still strangers drawn to each other despite good sense. But this time, their meeting involved more than passion. It involved Drew and a test to which he would not subject Blair.

A test he couldn't hope to win.

Because if she had balked before, what would she say now? Would she believe him or Drew? To believe him, she'd have to be willing to believe there was at least the possibility that her own brother was involved in embezzlement and had set him up to take the fall. That Drew Davenport, with his pristine reputation and more money than Michael could even understand, would be involved in something so vulgar. Or would she believe the more likely scenario: Michael Alvarez, of modest means and modest family, had wanted money to the point that he would go against everything he held dear?

Michael knew which version sounded more realistic. Drew, the wholesome all-American heir to a banking fortune, wouldn't become involved with bank employees Hector Ramos and Victoria Hart in the illegal transfer of funds. Michael had clear-cut evidence tying Ramos to crime. Victoria Hart was a little doubtful, but only because she'd saved his life by calling an ambulance. Either she or Ramos could have shot him, gotten the flash drive that contained the evidence he'd collected that far, and walked away leaving him to bleed to death. But Hart had called the ambulance when she'd found him wounded.

And if Drew wasn't involved, then who, within the Bureau, was? Bill Pride, his contact officer, knew where the flash drive was hidden. Michael's apartment had been ransacked. Bill wouldn't have had to do that.

Drew would. It always came back to Drew. Because Drew had more knowledge of the case than anyone other than Bill.

Even more damning, Drew's name had appeared many layers deep within the bank records, where nothing short of a thorough drilling down could find it.

With Drew involved, Michael had to stay away from Blair. But if things were different, if he were a different man, he'd walk into her room right now and love her.

The way he should have before. With more honesty than before. He'd passed up the opportunity to talk to her, to tell her what was going on with him. Back then he couldn't face his brother's death. Blair had been an anchor in a time of grief. He'd been afraid to voice his feelings. Instead, he'd tried to bury them.

And now, as he tried to forget, all he could do was remember that hot, bright day so long ago.

* * *

Six years earlier

The catamaran's bright yellow and red sail fluttered in the breeze. Michael found pleasure in showing Blair how to take the sleek little cat skimming across the water.

He loved the way she leaned back against him, the way her hair blew about them.

But what he really loved was her faith in him, in his ability to guide the tilting cat. To have her trust him as they went tripping across the flat water.

By the time they got back to her grandmother's it was dark. Alice Davenport's car was gone and they found a note, taped to the door, explaining that a good friend had had a heart attack and that she would be gone overnight. She would call and let Blair know when she'd be back.

Michael instantly picked up on Blair's nervousness as she let them into the empty house. Did she think he expected sex after barely two days? He nearly laughed, but sobered because he knew he'd wanted her from the first moment he'd seen her. Only he wanted to fan her hair out on a pillow and savor her, be gentle with her.

He groaned.

"What?" she asked after closing the door behind them.

Fighting to control the spiraling emotions he knew would destroy the hard won peace he'd found since meeting her, he said, "You need to soar, enjoy life, take chances. You were meant for it."

"I had a wonderful time. How did you learn to fly and sail?"

"My stint in the army gave me lots of opportunities all over. My brothers ... and I all learned to sail and fly." But even that response took him to places he didn't want to visit. Dark places where loss and anger threatened to engulf him and destroy what he'd found with Blair.

"You said your family's from Argentina. When did you move here?"

Safer ground. "I was fifteen. My father's a mechanical engineer. He got a job with an American company. My mother was happy. She's American."

"How did you meet John?"

This one was too close. Michael looked away. "We met through his work. Before I went to work for the Bureau."

"How long have you been with the FBI?"

"This is my second year."

"Two years less than Drew."

"Yes."

"Why the FBI?"

"It seemed like a good fit after the army." He shrugged, trying to put distance between himself and his answers. "It worked out."

Blair must have picked up on his reticence, because she changed the subject. "Are you hungry?"

"Starved," he replied, relieved they would move on to something else, some safer ground.

Blair opened the refrigerator, scanned the contents and turned back toward him. "How about peanut butter and jelly sandwiches?"

"There is nothing more awful than peanut butter and jelly."

She stared at him as if he'd lost his mind. "How can you not like peanut butter?"

"It sticks to the roof of your mouth."

"But it's good."

"No, it's awful." He stepped behind her. "Let me see what you have." He looked at the contents of the refrigerator, aware that he was trying too hard to make things light. "Here. I'll make you dinner."

He made an omelet full of tomatoes, onions and bacon, topped with grated cheese. They ate every morsel, laughing and talking over the old rock 'n roll station Michael had found on the radio. When they finished, his better self decided he'd better leave. Fast.

Getting involved would be a mistake. Whatever

happened between them would mean more than just being involved. He was in no position to give her anything but a good time. She was too young and too inexperienced to understand the limits of what he had to offer. He couldn't afford softer emotions, not if he intended to deal effectively with David's death, not if he intended to prove he could do the assignment he'd worked so hard to get.

Soft music filled the kitchen. Blair watched him with a combination of shyness and passion he sensed simmering beneath her caution. Every reason he'd given himself for not getting involved flew out the window. He could handle this. He could give her fun and pleasure, nothing more. Maybe it would be enough for her. It had to be for him.

"Dance with me," he said, knowing she should refuse, afraid she'd agree.

She looked at him with slightly wary green eyes and he almost walked away. Then she stood, took his hand and slid into his embrace, the fit so perfect Michael nearly stumbled.

He should have known then what would happen, where it would end.

When he bent to kiss her, she melted against him. Rod Stewart belted out *Tonight's the Night* and he was lost.

Chapter Seven

The present

Blair peered into the starlit darkness and made out the shape of the canoe, still partially hidden by dried sea grass and tumbling vines. They'd agreed to leave the island early, but Michael had pulled her out of a restless sleep long before the agreed upon four A.M. For one betraying moment, she'd thought he'd come to finish what they'd started on the deck.

She watched him uncover the canoe. "We can't leave now. There's not even a glimmer of dawn. It's crazy. We should wait until there's more light. We're likely to bump into the Marine Patrol on the bay."

"Blair, they'll have lights. We'll see them a mile away," he said. "Besides, if we wait, the tide will be against us."

His assessment of the situation made Blair clamp her mouth shut. He was right, of course. She'd known that when she crossed, or rather she'd gambled she was right. Michael would know. She protested when he insisted on paddling, even though her arms were too sore from all the raking and her own trip across. But, as usual, there was no arguing with him. His only compromise was to say nothing as she picked up the spare paddle and helped. Moments later they were moving across the darkened bay, bouncing on the choppy water.

They could see anything coming at them. A tug pushed a barge a good distance away, its lights making it look like a Christmas tree.

"It's pretty, isn't it?" he asked, echoing her thoughts.

"Yes, it is." She wondered how either of them could think of beauty at a time like this. She should be terrified; afraid they'd drown, or worse, get shot by one of the men who wanted Michael.

Ahead of them, the mainland loomed dark and imposing, the curve of Sunrise Cove, where they'd parted so long ago, clearly evident even in the darkness. They paddled the canoe to the shore, the sounds of the lapping waves beating a rhythm that matched the steady splashing of the paddles. Once the canoe scraped the sandy bottom, they jumped out and pulled it up into the pines.

"Where's the truck?" Michael asked as they donned shoes again.

"Over there." She pointed further into the tangle of trees and storm debris.

"Good girl."

She saw the white of his teeth when he smiled and felt unaccountably proud of getting his approval. They lifted the canoe and moved toward the hidden truck.

Once they'd loaded the canoe onto the trailer, they got in and Michael cranked the engine. The sound, so loud in the stillness of the trees, startled Blair. She searched the night, afraid of watching eyes. Michael let the engine idle a moment before shifting into gear, then pulled out from the protective cover of the trees onto the empty county road. He didn't turn the headlights on until they'd gotten away from Sunrise Cove.

As they drove through the darkened neighborhoods of Emerald Bay, past the turn to Blair's elementary school, she spoke. "I rented a car. You can take it."

She saw Michael shift in the seat beside her.

"I'm renting it by the week, so it won't be missed."

"What will you do for a car?"

It took her only a moment to think ahead. "I'll use this. My neighbor won't mind."

"Does Drew—"

"Drew doesn't know what I'm driving. He won't know what kind of car you're in."

He drove in silence until they reached an intersection with a still shuttered convenience store.

"Show me the way to your neighbor's."

Once there, Michael looked at the surrounding houses carefully, backed the trailer onto the driveway, and unhitched it from the truck. Blair walked to her house and opened the garage, where she'd left the rental. When he finished, they both stepped into the garage.

"What are you going to do now?" Blair asked, handing him the rental's keys.

"Straighten things out."

"How?"

"Better leave it alone, Blair. The less you know the better."

She shook her head, wishing she could deny the obvious.

This was just like before. No answers. No explanations. She knew the plans he'd made didn't include her, never mind that she'd spend the rest of her life wondering what if.

But that was pointless. She'd used all those emotions up years before. Michael did and thought as Michael saw fit. Explanations were not something he would give her, not really something she deserved. She had, after all, excluded herself from his life.

Morning sun breached the horizon, casting enough light so Blair could see Michael's face, his beard stubble dark against the paleness of his skin.

"I can take care of myself, Blair."

"You've done a great job so far," she said before she could bite back the sarcasm.

He laughed. That rich laugh she sometimes still felt in the dark of night when she missed him so terribly she could find no solace.

"Good God, Blair," he said, sobering, "I thought you were a sweet, compliant girl."

"I haven't been a girl in a very long time, and I'm far from compliant." She wanted to be angry with him, to hate him, to rid herself of the memories. "I'm not sure I was ever sweet."

She saw his eyes darken; saw the set of his mouth turn serious.

"No, Blair, you were sweet. Sweet as fire, burning hot." He touched her cheek with a gentle hand. "Sweeter than I deserved."

Before she knew what had happened, he stood before her, his face inches from hers. "You're sweeter now. Richer since you let the fire come up for air." His face descended toward hers, his strong, firm lips settled on hers.

Sweetness gave way to heat. The kiss consumed her, reminded her of so much. Of things she wanted to forget, especially her own weakness.

Then he released her, his dark eyes intent on hers. With his hands on her upper arms, he said, "Thank you, Blair. Thank you for blind belief." He pulled her close again and gave her a quick, hard kiss.

He walked quickly toward the rental, slammed the door shut and started the engine. Blair leaned against the garage doorframe, fighting the urge to go after him.

Michael backed out of the driveway and pulled onto the street.

He never looked back.

* * *

Things had certainly gone to hell in a hand basket, Michael thought. Two hours out of Emerald Bay, driving north, away from the hurricane-ravaged coast, he tried to focus on what he had to do. He was going to have to get some rest. If he didn't, he'd kill himself in a car wreck before he ever cleared his name. That would certainly be one way to finish this. If something else didn't finish him first.

He tried not to think of his mother and father and of how worried they must be. They'd already lost one son to law enforcement. But he wouldn't think about David now. Michael wished he could call and reassure his parents, but their phones had to be bugged. Unless his body turned up, Eddie and company would keep looking, as would Drew.

And there was Blair. Tempting him with lost possibilities. Another topic not worth broaching. Up ahead, Michael saw a small cinder block motel, a cheap wooden vacancy sign out by the dirt driveway. Across the road stood an old diner. As good a place as any to stop, sleep for a few hours, and grab a hot meal.

* * *

Blair sat down on her classroom floor and began sorting through the wet books on her bookshelf. She'd already gotten as many things as possible out of the way for the repair crew that would arrive tomorrow. Ellen Thompson had stopped by, looked helplessly into the rubble that had been her room, and had to be taken away, again, sobbing.

The sight of the first grade teacher had shaken Blair. Was she in danger of having so much of herself tied into something that could be destroyed so easily? Fear of just that had been part of the reason she'd refused Michael years ago. Now she wondered if she'd replaced Michael with teaching. With a classroom.

Angry with herself for even thinking about Michael again, she concentrated on the books.

"Miss Davenport?" Jason Petrie, the school secretary's eight-year-old son hurried through the open door and called to her.

"Yes, Jason?"

"There's a man looking for you." The small blond boy pointed to the dark hall behind him. "Mommy says Miss Allen's looking for you," he added in a conspiratorial whisper.

Assistant Principal Joanne Allen, a disapproving older woman waiting only for retirement, managed to make the wait awful for everyone.

Before Blair could get up off the floor, Miss Allen burst past Jason. "Blair, there's a man here for you." Slightly out of breath, she steadied herself against the doorframe. "You know you're not supposed to have visitors."

It wouldn't matter to Miss Allen that Blair wasn't really on school time. Rules were rules. She'd probably have a report in her file by tomorrow. She hurried to the door in time to see Drew moving down the hall toward her. He'd never come to see her at work.

Heart beating too fast, she refused to think about Michael. Drew would be able to see through her lies this time.

"Blair?" Miss Allen's piercing voice got Blair's attention. "Is this man your brother?"

"Yes, Miss Allen."

Miss Allen harrumphed, then eyed Jason warily. "I'll have to talk to your mother, young man. You're not supposed to be here." She turned toward Blair again. "You know you aren't supposed to conduct personal business at school." With that, she hurried off, Jason trailing behind.

"Is she always like that?" Drew looked at the retreating assistant principal.

Blair tried to laugh, but felt that it came out more as a gasp. "She doesn't like people. She loves rules."

"Rotten profession for her then."

"Is Mom okay?"

"Mom?" He looked puzzled for a moment, then nodded. "Of course, she's fine." He looked over his shoulder. "Where can we talk?"

"In here," she said, indicating her classroom. "Come on."

Once inside, Drew shut the door behind them. He looked around, slowly turning, taking in the broken window, the desks, all stacked to one side. Then he turned back toward her. "Where have you been?"

"What?"

"Where have you been? I've been calling to check on you since yesterday."

Blair blanked her mind of anything but what she must say. "I've been here."

"I went by your house late last night. I called all day yesterday. Your phone rings and rings. Your cell phone, too."

"The phone company doesn't know when the house phone will be up. It's the lines," she explained. "The cell phone works sometimes, but most towers are down."

"I called the school and they put me on hold. I waited forever before I gave up. When I came by, I couldn't get in."

Blair thanked heaven that the front office had put him on hold instead of telling him she wasn't there, and for the first time saw a good side to Miss Allen. "There's not much staff here during the summer. The best thing to do is to leave a message."

He looked at her pointedly, as if trying to read her. Blair struggled to meet his gaze.

"I wanted to see how you were."

Breathing deep, she said, "Well, I'm fine. I'm going to find out when they're going to let people on the island again. I'll check on the house."

"I'd rather you didn't go alone—"

The shrill beep of Drew's cell interrupted his words. He pulled out his phone. "Is there a land line phone I can use? I can get texts, but, as you said, calls are iffy."

"The teacher's lounge would be the best, I suppose." She led the way down the hall, then through the office to the tiny lounge. They waited while another teacher used the single phone. When she finished, Blair ushered Drew past the vinyl-topped table. He picked up the receiver, then turned back toward Blair. "Can you shut the door for me, please?"

"It won't keep anyone out," she warned.

Impatience flashed across his face. "Make sure no one walks in on me."

Of course. This was business. "Oh," she said. "Okay."

Blair walked through the doorway, pulling it shut. Then she leaned back on it.

She could hear what Drew said.

* * *

Michael pulled the baseball cap lower onto his forehead and stepped through the torn screen door of the diner next to the motel. He'd slept for four hours. Hunger had awakened him.

He nodded to the woman behind the cash register and walked into the dingy diner. Looking around, he saw a mix of people: those displaced by Nell, truckers, wanderers. This was his element, blending in something he'd learned long ago, before he learned to speak perfect English. Fifteen-year-olds named Miguel learned quickly to accept being called Michael and to be rougher and harder when necessary with schoolmates. Survival meant knowing when to give in, when to fight back.

This was the fight of his life. He wouldn't give up on clearing his name. He couldn't let himself or his family down. David had died while undercover, gathering evidence against a drug smuggling ring. Michael refused to let his parents lose another son. He smiled grimly at the limited menu and wondered why he thought he'd be able to get away when his brother hadn't.

But David hadn't had the miracle of dumb luck with which he'd been blessed. Lying in a hospital bed in Miami four weeks ago, shot through the diaphragm from left to right, he'd had enough internal injuries to make breathing, much less moving, painful. He'd just struggled into a sitting position, leaned forward toward the tray that held the latest issue of *Sports Illustrated*, when he'd heard the muffled sound of a shot against his pillow. He'd rolled off the bed, knocking over the tray, nearly knocking himself out from the shock of hitting the hospital floor. But there had been no second shot. He'd gotten himself up and gone to the door to look down the hall, but there had been no one. He was about to call Bill Pride, when Drew had walked in.

Michael still didn't know why he hadn't said anything to Drew. He'd let him think he'd gotten up to stretch, drawing his attention away from the ragged hole in the pillow, and talked sports, as if nothing had happened.

But Drew had asked questions, ones Michael didn't like. That had been when he'd first considered the possibility that Drew wasn't the friend he thought he was, and he'd decided to get away as quickly as possible.

From ingrained habit, Michael searched the diner for faces that looked out of place, anything that might spell danger. Survival instinct, one of his case managers had called it. He supposed it had saved him too many times to count.

Except that he knew Blair had saved him this time. Not once, but twice.

"Take your order, mister?" the diner's waitress asked.

* * *

Blair spotted her rental car parked outside a shabby motel two hours outside of Emerald Bay. She pulled her neighbor's truck up next to it and got out. Short of pounding on the doors of the four rooms closest to the car she knew Michael had driven, she didn't know what to do. Drawing that much attention didn't seem like a good idea. Readjusting her ponytail, she made for the small cinder block building that housed the office.

"Afternoon," an older woman greeted.

"Hi. I'm looking for my husband. He checked in a few hours ago. Tall, dark hair."

"You must mean that Vega fella. Good lookin'." The woman, worn beyond her apparent fifty or so years, took a drag from her cigarette. "He's in number two." She blew out the smoke from her lungs, turned, and reached behind her, taking a key from a set of numbered nails. "Here's another key."

"Thanks," Blair replied.

She knocked on the door to number two and waited. A minute later she used the key and turned the knob. The room was empty, the bed in disarray, Michael's backpack, the one she'd given him when he'd left her at home, lay in a chair next to a scared wooden table. Beyond the bathroom door, an open vinyl shower curtain revealed a dripping shower head.

Michael had to still be here. Blair walked to the single window and peered outside. Across the highway stood a diner. A car turned into the motel parking lot and pulled up to the office.

With dawning fear, Blair watched the heavyset man get out of the car and walk to the office.

Eddie's friend.

Heart in her throat, Blair moved away from the window. The motel manager would tell him where Michael was. She had to get away. One more look outside told her that the man was already walking toward the room.

She ran to the bathroom, trying desperately to find a way out or some place to hide. The window was too small to crawl through. The shower curtain looked so flimsy she discarded that as a hiding place. Back in the bedroom, the bed drew her attention.

With no time left to consider the wisdom of her choice, she shoved herself under the bed. The metal frame scraped her shoulder as she scooted toward the middle, anxious to be out of sight.

From the door came the sound of metal scraping on metal. One final movement put her in the middle of the bed, hair tumbling over her face.

After some more scraping sounds, the front door clicked open, then shut.

Eyes shut in fear and concentration, Blair matched the sounds of Eddie's friend moving around with her picture of the small room.

He walked to the chair that held the duffel bag. Blair heard him tearing through Michael's few things. He wasn't even trying to be quiet. Had the old woman not told him about her?

Blair lay in the oppressive closeness beneath the bed, her breath too fast and too loud. Finally, she dared open her eyes. The man, wearing scuffed deck shoes, walked past the bed. Blair tried to slow her breathing as she watched the disembodied shoes walk to the tiny closet.

She heard the scraping of coat hangers as the man pushed them aside. She saw when he tiptoed to reach up into the upper shelf, saw him walk into the bathroom, heard him push the shower curtain open wider. Thank God she hadn't chosen that as a hiding place.

He paused in the doorway of the bathroom, facing the bed. Blair's scalp tingled, her fists clenched tighter. Her breathing sounded harsh in her own ears. She watched the deck shoes draw nearer. He'd seen her. She closed her eyes, prepared to run.

The bed shifted. He'd sat down. Blair held her breath. In the deathly quiet, she heard tiny rhythmic beeps and realized he was using his cell.

"Yeah. It's me," he said in a smooth, dark voice. "I found where he's staying. He's not here. I can't find it." After a long pause, he continued. "No, there's nothing. Not a damn thing. He must have it on him." The man stood; the movement shifted the bed slightly. "I'll keep looking."

Then, in the stillness, Blair heard the sound of a key turning the door lock.

Michael.

The man strode quickly to the bathroom and pushed the door partially closed, leaving only a crack open.

Blair's breath caught. She had to let Michael know.

As she opened her mouth to yell out, it occurred to her that it might not be Michael who'd come in. She hadn't seen him, couldn't from beneath the bed.

No, it had to be Michael.

But just in case, she'd wait until she was sure.

Torn between wanting it to be Michael and not

wanting it to be him, she bit her lip.

Keys jingled in the quiet. If he would come closer to the bed, she'd know.

She looked toward the bathroom. From her vantage point, she could see through the crack. Eddie's friend watched silently, his arm down at his side. In his hand, he held a knife.

Blair's heart stopped. Still unsure who'd come in, she waited, then she recognized Michael from the running shoes he wore.

He was at the bathroom door and everything happened so fast, she didn't have time to warn him. But he'd known the man was there because he slammed the door back against him, knocking him out of sight. Blair heard him fall, saw Michael lean against the door.

Then they were grappling with each other, and Michael stumbled back into the room. The knife thudded against the thin carpet. Both Michael and the intruder lunged for it.

"Get back," she heard the man say as he grabbed the knife. Blair froze in her attempt to get out from under the bed. After a pause, he added. "Now."

The man stood, back toward her, the knife gripped firmly in his right hand, tilted upward, toward Michael.

"Make my life easier, man," the intruder continued. "Where'd you hide it?"

Voice calm, Michael replied, "Hide what?"

"The flash drive."

"What flash drive?"

"Don't give me crap, Alvarez. You Feds are big on evidence. Where'd you hide it?"

"If you know about Feds, then you know I turned it in."

"The hell you did. You got it somewhere."

Michael backed further into the bedroom, the man

followed.

"I'm a by-the-book sorta guy," Michael replied. "I turn in all my evidence."

The man laughed. "This time you didn't."

Blair shimmied out from under the bed, careful to stay too low for the man to see her. She was sure she'd been heard when her shoulder banged the bed frame, but he didn't turn. She crouched, trying not to so much as shift quickly. In her peripheral vision, she saw a plastic ice bucket sitting on the night stand. Exhaling softly, she inched toward it.

"You got me all wrong," Michael continued.

Afraid of what she might see, Blair didn't look up, but she could hear.

"In that chair," the man ordered, pointing to one by the door. "Let's see how cooperative you are in an hour."

Blair lifted the ice bucket, blood pounding through her body. As stealthily as possible, she walked up behind the man, sure the hammering of her heart would give her away. She could have sworn Michael didn't see her, so intent was his look on the stranger.

Behind the man, she raised the flimsy bucket. He turned.

In a blur of movement so quick she didn't see what happened, Michael raised his arm and the man lunged forward. Blair swung and hit the intruder on the cheek. The knife fell to the floor. Michael's fist connected with the man's jaw. He fell back, his head banging hard against the floor. Michael picked up the knife, then he looked up at her, his eyes blazing.

"What the hell are you doing here?"

The thunder in his voice matched exactly the anger on his face. To Blair's relief, he didn't come any closer to her, just stood stone still.

"I had to warn you."

"No you didn't. I can take care of myself."

"Like you did on the island?"

"Damn it, Blair." He seemed to be short of breath. "You need to stay away from me."

"But—"

He cursed, but his next words were soft, almost as if he was talking to himself. "What would have happened to you if I hadn't shown up just now?"

"He didn't see me."

"And you enjoyed being under the bed at the mercy of this son of a—"

"He didn't see me," she repeated, confused by his stillness.

"Jesus, Blair! Don't you understand? He could have killed you and it would have been my fault. For a woman who couldn't say goodbye fast enough six years ago, you keep hanging on!"

Chapter Eight

The words hurt. Because they were true. She had hung on throughout the years. She'd never forgotten, never stopped secretly wishing for a second chance, and yet never had the courage to do anything about it.

"Get out of here before this guy comes to," he said.

The breathless quality of his voice puzzled her. "Drew knows you're here."

Sweat trickled down Michael's temple. "Did Drew tell you that?"

"Of course not. I overheard him. You have to leave. Now."

He glanced at the still-open door. "Your truck out there?" His words came too fast, his breathing choppy.

"Yes."

"Drive straight back to Emerald Bay."

"Don't you understand? They know you're here!"

"Damn it, Blair, I know that." But there was no force behind the exclamation. He seemed out of breath. "I don't know who the hell Eddie's friend is. But where Drew won't hurt you, this guy will." He glanced down at the fallen man.

Michael swayed and for the first time, Blair noticed the grip he had on his shirt-front, beneath his slightly open wind breaker. She stepped closer and opened the jacket. A dark, wet stain spread across the bunched cotton of his shirt.

Blood.

"Oh my God! What happened?"

As she asked, she caught sight of the knife in Michael's hand. Blood covered the lethal blade.

"I need a towel," he said quietly.

Blair ran to the bathroom and grabbed two towels. When she came back, Michael had closed the door and was making his way to the chair. He eased down, his hand pressed to his side, his head leaning back. Blood oozed from between his fingers.

On her knees in front of him, Blair made a pad of one towel and began unbuttoning Michael's shirt. "Let me see," she said, "let me get to it."

He released his grip on the shirt and Blair pulled the shirt open. She had to wipe away blood to see the wound, an inch over the waistband of his jeans and well over to his left side, over the still healing surgical incision. She pressed a striped towel down on his warm flesh and looked up. "Why didn't you say something?"

"Get out, Blair."

"You are a complete idiot!" A rush of fear made her blurt out the words. "What were you thinking, trying to get rid of me?"

He closed his eyes. "This guy's going to wake up."

He'd been thinking of her. Trying to protect her at his own expense. She had to pull herself together, think for them both. This wasn't about second chances. This was about his life. Pressing against his side, she asked, "Do you have your gun?"

A weak laugh, followed by a gasp, came from Michael. "I didn't know you were blood-thirsty."

She didn't either, but at this moment, if that man regained consciousness and she could get her hands on a gun, she was pretty sure she'd use it.

She lifted the towel. The cut hadn't stopped bleeding. It had to be deep. He had to have stitches.

"We need the gun for protection."

"I have it," he said.

"We need to go."

Sweat covered Michael's ashen face. "Get me to the car."

"You need help. A doctor. I'll take you."

"I can't go down to the local emergency room." The words, deep and slow, rumbled from his throat.

Blair looked down at the towel, now soaked in blood. "You're losing too much blood."

Michael raised his head off the back of the chair, held the wet towel away from the wound, and stared down.

"It's too much blood," Blair repeated. "We have to get you help." She grabbed the second towel and pressed against him as his head fell back onto the chair again.

"Remember John's airfield?"

Blair looked up at him. "Yes."

"Can you get there from here?"

"Will going there help you?"

He nodded.

"Then I'll get you there." If it meant help for him, she had to.

Michael was already standing. With blood-smeared fingers, he took a gun from his back, placed it on the chair, and began undoing his brown leather belt.

"What are you doing?"

"Grab the backpack." He pulled the belt free.

When she stared, he prompted, "Hurry."

She snagged the blue bag, turned back, and found that he'd made a thick pad of the second towel and was wrapping the belt around himself to keep it on his wound. He wobbled, unsteady as he walked to the bathroom and washed his hands.

"What in the world are you doing?" She hurried to his side.

"Can't go out with blood all over me." His breath was coming quicker now. He turned, nearly overbalancing himself.

Blair grabbed his arm in an effort to steady him.

"Get me a clean shirt," he said in a whisper, balancing himself against the wall.

Somehow, they got the bloody shirt off and a clean shirt on him. Blair had to fasten the buttons because Michael was busy holding the towel tighter to his side. He insisted she put his bloody shirt and the towel in the plastic bag from the trash can, then place both inside the backpack. Once he got his jacket back on, he grabbed his gun.

"Let's go," he said, slipping the gun beneath the shirt into the back of his jeans, on the other side of his wound. "Bring the bag."

Terrified, Blair did, then grabbed his right arm.

"No." He pulled free. "On my left."

She wasn't going to be able to do this. What made her think she could help him?

Stepping behind him, she took his left arm and they made for the door.

"Mrs. Vega?" The female voice from beyond the closed door nearly stopped Blair's heart. It was the clerk.

"Yes?" she replied, throwing a quick glance at the man still unconscious on the floor.

"Can I talk to you?"

Michael opened the door enough for them to see the motel manager. "Something wrong?" he asked, holding on to the doorframe and blocking the view of the room.

"No, no. Just wanted to—" She paused, catching sight of Blair. "You goin' with your brother?"

Confused, Blair replied, "My brother?"

The woman squinted at her. "Fella I sent your way."

"No," Michael said, "she's not going with him."

Blair felt a tremor run through Michael's body.

"I don't normally meddle, you know."

Michael nodded. Blair couldn't understand how he kept himself upright.

"So I didn't know what to do," the manager continued.

"About what?" Michael asked.

"I told that man which room you and your wife was in. He said he was your brother-in-law, worried about you, he said. But he was nervous and, well, after this phone call I just got, I thought I'd better see what's goin' on."

"What phone call?"

"Marv O'Neil from over the Sheriff's office called. Said they're looking for a fella who's on the run."

"What did you tell him?" Michael asked.

"I told him I'd go check to see if the fella I talked to was still here." She moved her head to one side, trying to see around Michael. "Was that your brother-in-law?"

"Yeah, but he left. We won't trouble you anymore."

"Thank you," Blair said, hoping to hurry the woman along.

"You take care. You never know what kind of trouble you can run into." She gave then both a long hard look, one Blair was afraid would reveal Michael's bleeding side, but the woman turned and walked down the row of rooms, away from the office.

"Let's go," Michael said in an implacable voice.

Once in the pickup, Blair pulled out onto the highway, traveling south, back toward Emerald Bay. Michael, his head against the seat, sat immobile next to her. The only time she'd been to John's airfield, they'd come from Emerald Bay. She didn't drive this way often, but she thought she remembered where the turn was. Twenty minutes later, she passed it.

"To the right up here," Michael said once she'd made a U-turn on the deserted highway.

He directed her with mumbled left and right instructions, past the airfield. Quick glances at Michael revealed he was still resting his head against the back of the seat. His lids fluttered open. "That house," he said, pointing to a small, neatly kept, shingle house.

She turned back to Michael.

He had lost consciousness.

* * *

Elena Rodriguez looked like a sex goddess. Her dark hair tumbled down her back; her rich complexion glowed. Blair still wasn't quite sure how Elena had known to come rushing out, but there had been no doubt that she knew Michael. Concern had clouded the beautiful woman's features when she took one look at him.

But Blair didn't notice Elena's looks until after she'd sewn Michael up and bound his wound, partly because it took so much effort to understand Elena's broken English.

"I give him injection. You give him capsules." Blair accepted an envelope bulging with what appeared to be pills. "He must drink liquids. Today, tomorrow, next day maybe. Then, when he is hungry, red meat." She snapped a leather attaché closed. "Okay?"

"Yes." Blair bent over Michael, who lay on a floral couch, and pushed aside a lock of hair that had fallen over his forehead. "Why is he still unconscious?"

Elena seemed to analyze the way Blair touched Michael. "He will wake soon," she said abruptly, picking up the wash cloth and towel she'd used. "You will not leave him."

"No, of course not."

Elena nodded, seemingly satisfied. "I will give gauze to change for you."

Blair was beginning to understand the logic of Elena's English. "Can he be moved?"

"Juan and me will take you. He take truck to your house. He say car rent will be return, like that." Elena snapped her fingers, and bent to touch Michael's cheek. He didn't stir. "No one will know."

Blair nodded, her concentration on Michael's inert body.

Elena looked at her for long silent moments. "You are *la mujer ¿no?*" Elena asked.

"The woman?"

"The one who break his heart."

Blair wanted to shake her head, but felt pinned by Elena's dark eyes.

"*No importa.* No matter. You help him now."

Blair, aware she'd been judged but redeemed through helping Michael, couldn't resist her own curiosity. "How do you know Michael? Why are you helping him?"

"Because he save Juan." she replied. "He is ... *muy valiente.* How you say?"

"Very brave?"

"Ah, *sí.*" A spark of humor lit her eyes. "Also, he is *muy guapo.*"

"Handsome?"

"*Sí*, but we will see if he is shy, no?" She knelt next to Michael and began unfastening his blood-stained jeans. "I will wash his clothes, okay?" She didn't wait for Blair's reply. "You help."

* * *

Michael hurt. Everywhere. The most persistent pain came from his side, at his waist. Confusion blocked his efforts to understand why he felt so bad.

Then he remembered. He grabbed at his side and felt the thick bandage.

"You're safe." Blair spoke from a chair beside the couch where he lay.

She might have run like hell six years earlier, but she had helped him this time.

"Go now."

"You need help."

He should thank her by making her leave. He should insist.

But just one look at her stopped him. Maybe she had more spirit than good sense, but she was tenacious.

That tenacity had saved his life.

His mouth seemed unwilling to cooperate with his brain. Exhaustion pulled at his consciousness. Blair's face faded. His last thought was that he didn't have on any clothes. He started to demand she explain, but got no further than the thought.

* * *

Bright sunshine peeked through a crack in the blinds. Dust motes danced in the narrow rays.

Michael felt his side with care. It didn't hurt any worse to touch it, but there was no point in taking a chance, so he didn't press hard.

He looked around. Not Elena's house. This was an elegant bedroom. The bed beneath him was wide, the cotton sheets soft and cool. A small black and chrome table with matching chairs dominated a sitting area. A wet bar—chrome, of course—filled an entire wall. He struggled to raise his arm to check the time, but he wasn't wearing his watch. A quick glance down told him he only wore boxers. In front of the window, overlooking a garden, he saw jeans and a shirt draped over a chair.

With considerable effort, he rolled to one side and swung his legs over the edge of the bed. The bedside table, a modern looking black one, held his Glock.

Shaking, sweat rolling down his back, he stumbled to the chair and struggled into his jeans. He'd managed to pull them up before the door opened.

If it had been Eddie and his cohorts, he'd be a dead man. The Glock was just out of reach.

But it was Blair, dressed in shorts and a long-sleeved T-shirt. She carried a tray.

"You shouldn't be up."

He smiled at that, at his own weakness. "I'm not."

"You should have stayed in bed."

"And get caught with my pants off?"

She stepped in, leaving the door open behind her. "You certainly fought hard enough to keep them on."

Surprised at the mirth in her voice, he paused in his struggle to zip the jeans while seated. When he looked up at her, she was smiling.

"You would have thought Elena and I wanted to have our evil way with you."

He felt a flush creep up his cheeks. "I like to take off my own clothes." He sounded like an idiot. What he should have said, what she understood, given her next words, was that he liked to be in control.

"You were in no shape to do anything."

"I'm better now." Determination brought him to his feet. Dizziness brought him right back down. "Why are you still here?"

"I had two choices. I could let you fall flat on your face, or I could help." She paused. "Besides, after discovering how sensitive you are about dropping your pants, I was intrigued."

She seemed to be waiting for a reply, so he made the effort. "Don't expect me to thank you."

"Elena said you'd be crabby." She crossed the room and put the tray on the table.

"Where are we?"

"In Tampa. In a house that belongs to Elena's cousin. John and Elena flew us here."

"I don't remember a damn thing," Michael said, preparing to make another effort to stand.

"You were pretty out of it," Blair replied, then added. "She's very beautiful,"

"That's what John thinks."

Blair nodded slowly. "Oh."

Despite the dizziness, he fought a smile. He couldn't help but like the knowledge that she'd shown a little jealousy.

Then he sobered. "You'd better get back before you're missed."

"School's not in. No one will miss me."

"What about Drew?"

"He won't miss me."

"And if he does?"

"He knows the phones are a mess. Besides, it's not as if we talk to each other often."

He realized he was too weak to argue. "What's to eat?"

"Soup. Juice." She paused before adding, "Jello."

"Elena and her liquid diet."

Shadowed green eyes met his from across the room. "You've been like this before. With her."

He could have told her how Elena had saved his life once. How she'd kept him from bleeding to death from a gunshot wound to his thigh during an operation gone bad—the one that saved Juan from certain death. How in his delirium he'd thought Elena was Blair. How the beautiful woman couldn't practice medicine despite her medical degree because she couldn't speak English well enough. "Yes."

Blair stared at him, her face unreadable. Then she stepped forward. "I'll help you back to bed."

He didn't want her help. He wanted her gone before she got hurt. Before he got so used to her presence that letting her go would rip his heart out again.

But he couldn't get out of the damn chair.

He felt her arms around him, careful of his side, and used what little strength he had left to lever himself up. Stumbling back to the bed, Blair's perfume, a subtle mixture of vanilla and soap, brought back waves of memories—light, fun ones, blazing hot ones.

He groaned.

"Did I hurt you?" Blair asked, steadying him as they stood next to the bed.

Michael stared down at her upturned face and wondered if she could see his answer.

"The bed's behind you. Just sit back."

Stubbornly, he stood, legs braced apart, an arm around Blair's shoulder. "Go home, Blair. This is no place for you."

"Elena helped you. You didn't chase her away."

"I needed her help. I don't need yours."

She looked up at him again, this time with a quizzical half-smile. "You don't?"

He tried to straighten, despite the pulling at his side, despite the very real possibility his knees would buckle. "I could have gotten back to bed on my own."

Michael thought he'd won when her half-smile turned into a frown. Then the room spun and he struggled to ease back without hurting himself.

* * *

Blair stood in the kitchen, stirring a pan full of chicken noodle soup. She had never felt jealous in her entire life. There simply had been nothing to be jealous of. She had her parents' love, she had friends, had been engaged.

But right now she was jealous. Even though Elena and John were a couple, she had seen how well the woman knew Michael. She had helped him before. When Blair herself should have been there for him.

There was no one to blame but herself. She'd made the choice that ripped a common future from Michael and her. The emptiness of the past six years was her own doing. Her refusal of Jim Andrews, whom she'd been expected to marry, who'd seemed so right for her, had come too late to save Jim's feelings and her parent's embarrassment. But it had been the only choice she had when she realized she still wanted Michael. She'd simply figured it out too late.

Sweet Jim who'd promised a life in the suburbs, children, summer vacations, and more importantly, "normal," whatever that was. All those things she'd wanted as she'd watched her parents endure their marriage.

While she still pined for Michael and the heady passion of his loving. Michael, with whom life would have been an exhilarating ride, each day fraught with danger and insecurity. Never knowing anything beyond what he was willing to tell her. Never knowing if he'd come home. Knowing that nothing about Michael and herself would be mundane unless she made it so—worked at it.

Her parents' marriage had been a struggle. Her father's work and social schedule was not one with which her mother could cope, despite her desire to do so. As Blair grew older, she knew she wanted so much more for herself.

She should have shown more courage, been more willing to take a leap of faith. She should have understood that there were things Michael would never tell her. Instead, she'd thrown away the love of her life.

A tear tickled down her cheek and she swiped at it.

But she was different now, realized her failings, her bad choice. Michael had changed, too. He'd spent six years doing what he loved. Six years without the constraints of a woman of little courage.

She poured the soup into a bowl and prepared a tray. Elena's cousin certainly had high-priced taste. Expensive china and flatware graced the bright airy kitchen. The house, a little too modern for her, was filled with decorator-style furnishings.

Michael had quickly fallen into a restless sleep. Blair made sure his foray out of bed had not ripped his stitches, and, after seeing he'd quieted, decided he needed nourishment.

Now he lay on the white sheets, his dark hair tousled, his chest bare, his eyes watching.

"You're awake. Good."

"I don't suppose you have real food there."

Blair stepped into the room. "Chicken noodle soup."

"Funny, you don't look like my mother."

Blair felt his perusal and struggled for a reply. "Elena said liquid first."

"Elena's never had to survive on liquid."

"But you have."

His dark eyes met hers. "Yes, Blair, I have. That's the kind of life I live. The kind of life I like." His voice sounded hard.

She had no response for that, so she tried for humor. "You like being hurt?"

Michael sighed. "You know what I mean."

"Drink the soup, Michael," Blair said putting the tray down next to his gun on the table. "Can I put this in the drawer?"

"Give it to me."

She picked up the gun, handed it to him and watched him put it under the spare pillow.

Then he rolled to one side, bracing himself to sit up. Blair leaned over and helped.

"Don't let me get used to having you around," he said.

Blair straightened once he rested against the headboard, prepared to tell him he needed her, but stopped herself. Did she want him to need her? Did she really want a second chance?

He looked at her levelly before adding. "It's something you'll regret."

* * *

They spent two days between bursts of conversation fit for strangers and uneasy silences. Michael wished there were words that would place her out of harm's way. He thought of plenty, but couldn't bring himself to be that cruel again. Blair cooked, changed his dressing, gave him his pills.

And while he regained his strength, courtesy of steaks and rest, Blair seemed remote and unwilling to talk about anything but his health, the weather and the news. He knew she'd told friends and her mother that she was visiting in Atlanta before leaving with him for Tampa. When he asked if Drew had tried to contact her, she told him she didn't know. Her home phone still didn't work and she hadn't brought her cell, which was good since any calls on it could be tracked.

They couldn't continue like this. He couldn't. This morning, he'd decided to be firm, but kind. She had to go.

She brought him a plate and a glass of orange juice as he sat at the table in the kitchen, her hair brushing the shoulders of a Mickey Mouse shirt. He supposed she'd had to buy some things since she couldn't go home. The clothes she'd been wearing didn't look like the sort of thing he'd ever seen her in. Blair Davenport wasn't flashy, she had good taste. This outfit looked like it had been picked piece-meal, as she needed things.

To stop himself from thinking about her looks and her clothing, he spoke. "Is that bacon I smell?"

"And eggs. Should send your cholesterol levels into the danger zone."

"But I'll die a happy man."

The juice nearly sloshed out of the glass when she released it. Her green eyes flashed as they zeroed in on him.

That one look spoke volumes. Her face paled. Fear. For him.

Michael didn't want to see it, didn't want to acknowledge it.

The air vibrated with unspoken tension. He grabbed for the glass in an attempt to steady it, to steady himself.

His fingers closed over Blair's hand. The contact singed him. He brought his other hand up slowly, to see if she'd object, to Blair's arm, to the pulse point at her throat, to the back of her neck. To draw her face down to his, savor.

Want.

Her lips, cool and soft, flowered for him. For a single instant he was aware of Blair's hands on his shoulders. Then all was heat and promise.

With fingers eager to feel her warmth, he pushed his hands into the thickness of her hair, to hold on. To never let go.

Unbearable hunger thrummed through him as her mouth took in his desire and re-doubled it. Tongues touched, feasted. There didn't seem to be enough air, enough time, enough—

He fought for control, for something to distract him from what he wanted more than anything.

Pulling back, he found the strength to push her away gently.

Because he loved her.

Chapter Nine

Blair stumbled back, the glass, the food, forgotten. He'd robbed her of breath, of reason, in a heartbeat.

"You need to go, Blair. I'm getting stronger. I'll be back to normal soon."

She stared, mute, at his mouth.

"It would be easy to make—have sex. It was good before."

Blair wanted to crawl into a hole as his words pierced her heart.

His dark eyes held hers. "I don't think either of us wants that without the emotion."

She wanted to tell him it wasn't true, but couldn't. Six years ago she'd loved him so much there was no question they'd make love. Now she didn't know. She shook her head.

He said nothing, cool, dark eyes locked to hers.

Her thoughts raced. She'd wanted to love Jim Andrews, such a nice man. She'd felt like she'd betrayed something sacred when she'd been with him. Seeing Michael made her realize she had.

Silence, thick and heavy, lay around them.

The phone rang, startling her. She met Michael's gaze.

"Answer it."

She reached for the shrilling portable on the counter behind her.

Elena asked specific questions about Michael's

condition. Blair listened carefully, then handed the receiver to him and backed away. He watched her.

"*Hola*, Elena." He spoke in Spanish for a minute then stretched, wincing, to hang up the phone.

"I told her you were leaving today."

That nearly stopped her heart. She hurried to answer. "You can't manage on your own."

"I've managed before."

"Elena says you need to rest, regain your strength for a few more days."

"I can do that alone."

"You can't get up without falling down."

"I was ready to make love to you and I wasn't going to fall down!"

His words, his anger, cut through Blair's reserve. "You're sitting down, Michael."

"Damn it, Blair!" He pushed away from the table and stood. "This isn't a game." Grasping the back of the chair, his mouth a thin line, he continued. "There are people willing to kill me without a second thought."

"You—"

But it wasn't necessary for her to argue back. Michael sat back down, heavily, his eyes closed. Quick seconds later he looked up at her. Blair could see the effort he was making to look strong.

"You need me. Let me stay."

"Why?"

"Because I didn't before."

* * *

An uneasy peace settled between them and held for the rest of the day. Michael cursed the weakness of his own body, consoling himself with the knowledge that if he hadn't been shot a month ago, he probably wouldn't feel so bad.

He'd never thought in terms of getting hurt, only in

terms of what he had to do. Hell, he never thought beyond the job at hand. He'd done exactly the same thing with Blair. Sleepy from making love, he'd wanted more. Blair wasn't the type of girl who would simply go away with him. Blair was the kind of girl you married. So he'd asked.

And she'd turned him down.

The thought of her with another man made his head hurt.

And now she wanted to make up for saying no. She didn't know that her refusal was the best decision she'd ever made, that her high-society boyfriend could have given her what she needed.

Safety, security, life in her world, and 2.2 kids.

Not his kids.

* * *

"Bacon for breakfast again?"

"I bought a pound. We might as well eat it," Blair said, putting the plate down. Outside, clouds played at hiding the morning sun.

"Part of Elena's instructions?"

"She says you need protein."

"I need to get up and out of here."

Blair had been expecting this since they'd agreed, two days earlier, that she would stay. Michael had been in worse shape than she'd imagined because he hadn't done much more than sleep, occasionally walking around the house and stretching. Normally, he wouldn't have stayed put for a minute.

"There's a pool. It might feel good to get some sun."

"Which vitamin does Elena think that will give me?"

"D."

He laughed. After their awkward silences of the days before, the sound of it made her smile.

"Eat your breakfast. I'll bring you the swim trunks I

found in the pool house."

"Eat some with me," he said. "You might as well have some protein, too."

An hour later, Michael came out of his bedroom wearing black trunks, the bandage he'd changed himself startlingly white against his skin. Blair resisted the impulse to stand and help him into the lounger. But he didn't sit; he walked around the pool, proving he was stronger and didn't need her any more. She had to get used to the idea that within a day, two at the most, he'd leave her behind.

The blue water of the pool glistened in the morning sun. Away, to the west, storm clouds gathered. Around them, the lush, sculpted garden enclosed them in ever-increasing humidity.

"Has anyone come knocking?" Michael asked, sitting on the lounger next to hers.

"No, but the pool man called. I asked him to wait until next week."

"We'll be gone by then."

"Where?"

"You to your house, me, away."

Blair swallowed. She kept her eyes shut behind the sunglasses she wore. "Where?"

"Don't ask what I can't tell you."

"Same as before."

"No. Different. Before I should have told you. Should have explained how it would be. Now ... well, now it's a little more complicated."

"Why didn't you tell me before? Why did you want me to come with you if you didn't trust me?"

She thought he wasn't going to answer and opened her eyes.

He looked at her, his expression shuttered. "I wanted blind faith."

And she'd wanted a utopian dream no one, not even he, could give her.

* * *

Michael ate the roast beef sandwich Blair made him for lunch. He'd spent the morning between the bedroom and the pool, walking, stretching, and resting. He was stronger. Blair busied herself with something, Michael didn't know what. The silence between them grew as oppressive as the building afternoon humidity, yet he thanked God for it.

Because in that silence he turned over the bits and pieces of what he hoped would clear him.

Bank employees Hector Ramos and Victoria Hart were in charge of bank-to-bank transfers at the Miami bank that had been Michael's last assignment. Michael had proof positive of Hector's involvement in the theft of hundreds of thousands of dollars. Hector's weakness was gambling. A friendly man with a wife and children, he did not have the salary to cover the losses he took in a single night of gambling. That had triggered the extra push Michael had made to look at Hector's transfer figures. That's where he'd found discrepancies. Not big ones—little ones, as least for a while, over a long period of time. A year and a half ago, Hector only skimmed a thousand every few months. The take from the last week Michael had figures on was close to fifty thousand. The grand total had been close to a million dollars. Either Hector found it so easy that he increased his withdrawals, or something changed in his life.

Michael had downloaded Hector's transactions onto a flash drive, which he'd hidden in his apartment until he could give it to Bill, his contact officer. Based on that evidence, he'd reported that Hector was his prime suspect. Bill and Drew, who'd worked a similar fraud case, had agreed that someone would follow Hector.

Then Michael had been shot and the flash drive had vanished. He'd been sure that Hector had shot him and taken the evidence. Now he wasn't so sure. If Hector had the evidence, what was the guy in the motel after? There had to be someone else.

Drew wanted Michael, there was no doubt there. But could he really be the other player in the game?

Michael caught sight of Blair through the glass door that led from the living room to the pool. Sleek and perfect, she'd donned a simple green tank suit and was pulling her hair back into a ponytail. Drawn outside, he watched the graceful movements of her arms, the curves of her body. With a final tug at the band that held her hair, she dove into the pool and began a steady crawl across. On the other side, she made a racer's turn and came back.

He wished he could burn some excess energy that way. Wished he could join her in the pool. Wished he could give her a house like this: one she belonged in, where she fit and he didn't. Angry reflex had made him say things he shouldn't have said when she'd refused his proposal. He'd gone off to his undercover assignment— his opportunity to get the men who'd killed David—full of indignation at being used by a rich socialite. He held on to the anger that she'd been playing with him for about a week. That quickly burned away in the reality of what his life became: a deadly game to avenge his brother. Blair Davenport didn't belong in a world like that, didn't need it.

Which led him right back to Drew. Drew's name had been in one of the files he'd seen, but not copied. There had been a ten-thousand-dollar withdrawal wired in from Mexico. The name triggered a second look. And he found Drew's name again. Twice, for the same amount. Drew didn't need money. He was a Davenport.

He didn't live ostentatiously. He didn't flaunt what he had. As a matter of fact, if Michael had to guess, he'd say Drew lived within his Bureau paycheck. But it didn't change what he saw.

Then Michael made a mistake. Misguided loyalty to a friend made him keep quiet. He didn't tell Bill Pride, he didn't follow procedure. He was in the process of double checking figures, names, when he'd been shot.

But with the flash drive gone, when he woke up in the hospital, he had absolutely nothing to show for over six months of undercover work. Nothing except a bank account in his real name with an extra ten thousand transferred in from a Mexican bank.

To give Bill his due, he hadn't accused him outright of thievery, but Michael knew he was under surveillance, if not under arrest. After the shooting in the hospital, when he knew he couldn't trust Drew, he'd had no choice but to run.

Blair climbed out of the pool, drops of water gilded by mid-afternoon sun beaded on her face, her legs. She caught a finger beneath the right strap of the suit, adjusting it. Michael's eyes centered on her breasts. The thin material of the suit did nothing to hide them. He could picture them bare, the tips a dusky pink. Desire pooled in his body.

Caught in the movement of pulling the band from her hair, she looked through the sliding glass door at him.

She'd read his need correctly.

* * *

Blair grabbed her purse from the foyer table. "Be back in a while!"

She didn't wait for Michael's reply. She couldn't face him. She'd seen desire in his eyes when she'd stepped out of the pool and knew he'd seen it in hers. He knew how she felt. So when he turned away, she'd wanted to run to him and beg. Pride and self-preservation made her walk into her room, shower and dress.

Inside the rental car she'd gotten with Elena's help at the airport, Blair turned the air conditioner blower to high in order to fight the heat and humidity. It would storm soon. The beautiful greenery of the quiet neighborhood stirred in the increasing breeze. The vegetation and architecture might be different, but the atmosphere was that of her own home. Affluent.

She thought about Jim Andrews. Everyone had said they were perfect for each other. Both with the same background, the same friends. Sameness was what Blair had always longed for, what she thought would give them a stable, easy future, so unlike her parents' marriage.

Beth Davenport, until her marriage to Andrew Davenport, Sr., was nothing more than the hired help. And not really that. She was Grandfather Davenport's secretary's daughter. Her own mother had opposed the marriage. The only one who'd approved had been Grandma Alice, her father's mother. And God knew why she had, because she'd never explained herself.

Blair had grown up watching a man and woman who obviously adored each other, try to fit in the other's life, with their differing families.

She remembered the morning Michael asked her to marry him. She'd been shocked. Surprised beyond belief. Michael Alvarez wanted to marry her, wanted her to come with him? Her mind raced through the possibilities. She'd go with him. They'd continue as they had that week.

Then Michael told her he'd be undercover for six months, maybe a year. And he told her nothing more. She'd wanted answers. When would she see him? How dangerous was it? What was it? He said nothing except that he'd do his best.

His best to do what? To stay alive? To come back? To make a marriage work? After six months, he might decide that a fling with an inexperienced college coed wasn't for him. She couldn't hope to keep up with him. She couldn't hope to be as exciting as his job, as their week had been. If he lived—and the thought that he might not choked her—they'd spend their lives like her parents. She simply didn't have the courage for that.

But if she said no, she wouldn't have to wonder when he'd leave her to go to that life he loved. The life that filled a need in him she could never hope to fill.

She'd been a fool. She should have said yes. She should have risked because Michael Alvarez was worth it. She'd buried herself behind platitudes of what she thought she wanted and could handle.

But she had now. She wouldn't spend another six years full of regrets, missing him with every fiber of her being.

* * *

Wind blew against the window. Michael hoped Blair got back before the storm hit. According to the Weather Channel, they were in for severe thunderstorms.

He'd exercised, careful of his stomach and his side. The cold shower he'd taken had not brought the peace he craved. Neither had the nap he'd taken. Even in sleep he could see Blair standing, provocatively wet, by the pool.

Sweet Blair. She'd ruined any other woman for him. He'd tried to bury the wonder of that week, tried to burn her out of his system, with a woman who wanted to play at life.

Michael couldn't blame Blair for turning to that fiancé in order to get on with her life. She owed him nothing, yet here she was, risking so much to help.

Thunder rumbled in the distance. Michael heard the front door close, the car keys drop on the marble-topped table in the tiled foyer, and her footsteps.

* * *

Blair's heart hammered in her chest. Making a decision in the confines of the car had been one thing. Acting on that decision was another.

Michael had charmed her, overwhelmed her, before. This time she was going in with her eyes wide open, knowing what she was risking, making a decision based on what she'd learned in their time apart. No matter what happened after today, she'd know she made the right decision.

None the less, opening Michael's bedroom door was the most difficult thing she'd ever done.

Because he could refuse her. As she had him.

The knob turned, cold and stiff in her hand. Once she'd pushed the door open, she saw Michael lying on the bed, wearing nothing but a pair of khaki shorts, his legs crossed at the ankles.

She took a deep breath, yet her words came out as a whisper. "You were right. I want the feelings, the emotion." She inhaled a quick breath. "Do you feel anything for me?"

Long moments passed before she heard his rough answer. "That is the most fabulously stupid question I've ever heard, *corazón*."

If he hadn't used the endearment, if he'd said the words coldly, she would have shriveled and died. But Michael's words were hot with promise.

"The reason you stopped … um, wouldn't, ah … make love at the beach." Her voice wobbled. "I took care of that." Somehow she made her way across the room, dropped her purse on the fancy glass table beside the window, and fumbled inside. Finding what she'd bought at the drug store, she spread five of the ten small gilded packets from the box out on the table.

He smiled. "You have overrated expectations of my current physical condition."

Her purse fell off the table, scattering its contents on the carpeted floor. A flash of lightning lit the room. She peeled her eyes away from the window and risked looking at Michael.

What she saw lightened her spirit. Strong and sleek, his eyes alight with fire, he said, "If you plan to use any of those, you'd better come to me."

Ignoring the purse, grabbing the packages, she took the few steps necessary to stand beside the bed. Eyes locked to his, she dropped the condoms on the bedside table and kicked off her sandals.

In the charged light of the afternoon, Michael's words washed over her. "Undress for me, Blair. Let me see you."

Shivers ran up Blair's back. Indecision crowded her thoughts, despite her certainty of moments before. Six years ago, she'd welcomed Michael's love making, reveled in it. But she'd never initiated it. Couldn't remember that they'd ever taken the time to tease each other because the heat of their hunger always pushed them to hurry.

The sensual promise she read in Michael's eyes decided for her. Standing barefoot beside the bed, she unbuttoned the navy blue shorts and pulled down the zipper. They dropped to the floor and she stepped clear.

Michael watched Blair with a sense of unreality. She lifted her shorts off the floor and placed them on a chair. The high cut of her panties showed off the beautiful length of her legs. She turned toward him again, her eyes a sea green in the muted, stormy light of late afternoon. Her right hand began working the buttons at her throat, the collar of her white cotton blouse high. He saw her tremble as she moved down past her breasts. The blouse parted and the silky skin of her stomach appeared.

Desire, heavy and thick, surged through his body.

Blair shrugged out of the blouse and stood before him in her white panties and lacy white bra. Michael swallowed the lump in his throat.

But he reined in his passion when he saw her shift uncomfortably under his gaze. Swinging his legs over the side of the bed, his eyes steady on hers, he stood and walked toward her.

He could guess how much undressing for him had cost her. That single week had remained in his mind as an erotic feast, but he knew that Blair was basically shy. The heat of their union had broken down her normal barriers, but they hadn't seen each other in six years. He, himself, was a little worried about her expectations.

"You're beautiful, Blair," he said, placing one hand on her cheek. "Even more beautiful than before."

She closed her eyes and leaned in to his palm. He bent and kissed her shoulder, so warm. Then he could resist no longer. He pulled her in to his arms, loving the feel of her, so right, so womanly, against him. God, how he'd missed this. Her.

Pulling back marginally, he took her mouth with his. She opened immediately, her mouth welcoming. He plundered, feasted. She tasted of mint, of freshness, seething with wildness.

Breaking the kiss to look at her, he nearly fell to his knees. Her mouth, wet from his kiss, beckoned him. Her breasts, hidden by the bra, tempted him.

"Where does this thing fasten?" he asked, sure his voice had come out as a croak.

Her slim fingers touched her cleavage. With trembling hands, he fumbled with the fastener until it came free. The white lace parted and her breasts were bared for him. Plump, perfect, the tips already puckered. He bent and took one in his mouth, tonguing the delicious flesh, pulling at her. Her hands tangled in his hair, urging him closer as he moved to the other breast.

He buried his face against her, smelling her sweetness, feeling her fire. Straightening, he pushed the straps off her shoulders and watched the bra fall to the floor. He pulled her close again.

She ran her hands down his back, over his hips, pulling him even closer. The pleasure of her silken flesh against his tore through him. He adjusted their bodies until he rubbed, hard and insistent, against the notch at her thighs.

Her gasps filled the room, pushed at his control. Lightening filled the room. He pulled away, wanting to rein in his hunger, wanting to give her pleasure unimagined.

"Slow down," he said, but the words were intended for himself.

Blair stared at Michael with unabashed hunger. At his beautiful face, his incredible chest, the hard evidence of his aroused sex straining at his shorts. The touch of his hands caressing, rubbing, propelled her into action.

She stroked the crisp hair of his chest in search of his nipples. She circled with her thumbs, watched his eyes darken, felt the tiny nubs harden. Stepping close, she kissed the line of his collarbone, tasted his flesh, traced a path to his nipple. His groan, deep and masculine, reverberated through her. She kissed her way to his stomach, careful of the bandage. Straightening, she concentrated on the single snap of his shorts.

Rain slashed the window as she fumbled, her fingers

clumsy. The sound of his zipper caused shivers of anticipation to form along her skin. She could feel him, hard and heavy, against the backs of her hands. The parted material revealed blue patterned boxers. He pushed both boxers and shorts down.

Lightning washed the room in light as she touched him.

He kicked free of his clothes, his eyes fastened to hers.

"Maybe you should lie down." The sound of her voice, so tight, surprised her.

"Probably so," he said with a soft laugh. He pulled her toward the bed and stretched out, his incredibly aroused body hers for this moment in time. A feeling of power, of destiny, washed over her.

She straddled his thighs, her body aching for his. He pulled her over him, adjusting so that his erect flesh rubbed where she most wanted him.

Lightning crackled overhead, thunder rolled, wind and rain slashed against the window. Inside, heated breaths praised touches remembered. He nudged her thighs further apart and she rose over him. Moments later he was pushing inside her, driving, pulling gasps of pleasure from her.

He thrust upward, then froze, straining. In the stillness she tried to adjust to the invasion, tried to calm jittery flesh that hovered on the brink of release. She eased herself down more and felt his flesh leap inside her. He reached up and took a nipple into his mouth.

The pressure of him inside her, ready to burst, the pressure of his mouth, so tight, undid her. She slid into climax, moving her hips until the pleasure stopped her.

He moved, driving himself deeper, harder, faster. She fell forward, her breasts against his chest, his hands on her hips, controlling her movements. She felt the waves again as Michael's head fell back, his neck exposed to her.

His pleasure shuddered through her as the storm outside raged.

* * *

"How many of those did you buy?" Michael asked against Blair's neck.

"Ten."

"Why not more?"

"I didn't want you to think I was making demands."

His laugh rippled through their joined bodies. "*Niña*, right now, the thought of two is enough to deflate me."

He felt her hands explore his chest, felt her shift around him. Felt his instant response.

She smiled down at him. "Deflate you?"

Chapter Ten

Michael kissed Blair gently on the lips and rolled onto his back.

"Are you okay?" Blair asked against his shoulder.

"Mmhm," he replied, too lazy to talk.

She felt gently for the bandage at his waist.

"I haven't sprung a leak," he said, holding her hand.

Apparently satisfied, Blair scooted more fully against him, resting her head on his shoulder, one leg thrown over his. She sighed.

Tangling one hand in her hair, he began, "Blair—"

"Don't." She tensed in his arms. "Don't say anything about why or tomorrow. Please."

He wanted words. Needed those he hadn't spoken six years earlier. Words of love if not of commitment. But they would remain unspoken. She couldn't commit to the man who would ruin her brother.

She readjusted herself against him. "This is a place out of time. Let's leave it that way. No recriminations. No second guesses. We don't have the time for them."

Pushing aside his grim thoughts, he smiled against her hair. "I don't think I can manage more."

She elbowed him lightly. "You know what I mean."

He did understand. She didn't.

He turned his head slightly to rub a handful of her hair against his face and concentrated on the texture, the smell.

She pulled away and maneuvered herself so she

supported her weight on her elbows and looked down at him. He shivered at the sensation of her finger tracing a line from his brow, around his cheek, to his lips. "You are the most beautiful man."

"Blair, I wish—"

"No," she said, stopping him by pressing two fingers against his mouth. "If you have to talk, tell me about yourself." She paused and he knew she was going to ask something important. "Tell me what you didn't tell me before."

Michael kissed her fingers. Blair eased down beside him again. These words were his commitment to loving her, as much as the joining of their bodies had been. She had no way of knowing or understanding because he couldn't tell her about Drew. She'd shown her faith in him by helping him. He couldn't give her forever, but he could try to explain what happened before. He could give her that.

"I didn't tell you because it was so new I couldn't handle it. Part of it was—" he still couldn't explain it. Maybe the telling would make it clear. "My brother David was a year younger than me." He forced himself to take a deep breath. "Our parents used to say we were meant to be twins."

"You were close."

"Close and very competitive. Anything one of us did, the other had to do." He stared up at the ceiling. "From things as simple as playing soccer to jumping off bridges on a dare."

"So you both went into law enforcement."

Michael hoped he would be able to explain. "David joined the army." He'd never spoken the words, but knew his parents had thought them. "Just as I did." He felt Blair turn and tilt her head toward him. "Because I did."

She tucked herself closer.

"I got hurt pretty badly during an operation, and decided to get out because I couldn't do what I'd been doing. David finished his time and got out, too. I had already joined the Bureau, David applied and got in.

"I was always the one who got us into things. About the only thing David did without my having done it first was get married." Michael struggled to keep his voice smooth. "That and getting himself killed."

Beside him, Blair stiffened. "Oh, Michael—"

"His wife's name is Stephanie. She remarried last year." He took a breath. "I don't blame her at all." He'd surprised himself. "She and David wanted children. She'll have them now. She waited too long as it is."

"You blame yourself, don't you?" Blair sat up, pulling the sheet around herself. "You blame yourself because he joined the FBI."

"He wouldn't have done it if it weren't for me."

"That doesn't say much about your brother."

"He should have done something different." Michael shut his eyes. "Something safe."

"Like jumping off bridges and joining the army?" She looked down at him. "I don't know exactly what you did, but I know it wasn't safe. Even before that, it sounds to me like you were a pair of daredevils. I'd say he had to have some sort of excitement. Something with an edge of danger. Like you do."

"I could have picked something else."

"Come on, Michael! How long would you have lasted in a nine to five job? How long would David have tolerated that?"

Logically, everything she said made sense. He'd tried the same arguments on himself. Millions of times. He always came back to one fact. "He'd be alive." That seemed to silence her.

"How did it happen?"

"They needed someone whose Spanish was Argentinean. I wanted to do it, but the agency had me tied up with something else." He'd seen it as simple competition. Not life or death. How stupid he'd been.

"That smuggling task force Drew had worked on." She remembered.

"Yes." He sat up and leaned against the headboard. "David was free so they sent him. It went pretty well for a while. Then they made him."

"How?"

"The working theory is that he slipped up somehow, but we never really found out for sure."

"Did the men who did it go to jail?"

"They paid for what they did." But not enough. He couldn't tell her why those men deserved more than what they'd gotten. David had been tortured. That was one thing he'd sworn never to tell anyone. It preyed on him in the dark of night.

"Then David was avenged."

Michael laughed. He couldn't help it. Her words had taken him from the ugliness of his memories to the realization that he'd misunderstood this woman whom he loved. Revenge wasn't as uncivilized for her as he'd thought.

"What's so funny?"

"You are so fierce, *niña*." He leaned toward her and kissed her forehead. "And so very, very beautiful." He pulled her against him, thankful for the warmth of her body.

* * *

Blair stretched and listened to Michael, singing in the shower. This morning they'd woken in a tangled heap of bedclothes and warm limbs. She'd forgotten how hot he got at night, how he tossed the blanket off the bed.

How he sang, scrambling the lyrics.

She smiled and rolled over, looking outside. Yesterday's storm left behind cooler temperatures. They'd gone out by the pool at midnight, with all the lights off, and, crowded together on a lounger, stared up at the sky. Soft conversation, gentler touches, had led them into gentle passion.

"Do we have more bacon?" Michael, rubbing a towel through his dark hair, looked across the room toward her.

"Yes." Her eyes feasted on him. He'd already changed his bandage.

"Don't look at me like that, *querida*. You've built me up to destroy me with your demands?"

She laughed and couldn't remember feeling freer in ages. "We still have steaks."

He walked to the bed, nakedness of no concern, and bent to kiss her. "I'll cook the bacon. You'll need to make the steaks for lunch. I won't have the energy."

His promise made her smile. A hard kiss to her mouth and long, lingering caresses in all the right places, had her squirming. He wasn't unaffected.

"How will you cook bacon like that?" She leaned back on her elbows.

"I'll wear an apron."

"Make it asbestos, I don't want to risk anything to hot grease."

He rolled onto the bed next to her, laughing, and she made her getaway.

* * *

"You cheated." Blair's voice came to Michael at the same time he felt a tug on the seat of his jeans.

He was taking bacon from a skillet, his back to her. "I didn't think the apron would do much to protect me."

"Good thinking."

"Want some?" He turned and held a piece of bacon to her mouth.

She took a bite, crunching delicately, her eyes holding his. "Good," she said after swallowing.

And he remembered another time, another place where they'd shared food and love. He bent and took her mouth, tasting the bacon, feeling where her wet hair had dampened the cotton shirt she wore. He fought the temptation to take her back into the bedroom.

Pulling away from the intoxication of her mouth, he turned back to the stove. "Eggs?"

"No, thanks." He heard her move away. "I'll make toast."

Michael took cups from the cabinet and poured coffee for both of them. "Turn on the TV. Let's see the local weather."

Barefoot, she walked across the shiny kitchen and pushed a button on the small set. "It's a little early, yet, I think."

"Turn it down then. We'll turn it up when the weather comes on."

They ate in companionable silence, by moments exchanging simple conversation, by others watching the muted television. Blair took the plates to the sink then sat back down to enjoy one last cup of coffee.

"I'll need to go buy a few more things at the grocery store."

"Don't buy much." Michael hated seeing the cautious look take over her face. He tried not to think of what was to come. "We'll leave tomorrow."

"Where will we go?"

"You'll go home, Blair."

"What about you?"

"I have to clear my name."

"I can help."

"It's best that you don't." *Because I love you.* He wanted to tell her. Right then. He wanted to shout the words. To stop himself, he glanced at the television.

And saw Buddy Alcott, the FBI public relations liaison, speaking to a female reporter in front of the Miami office. Michael flicked the mute button on the remote, and Buddy's words cut across the silence of the kitchen.

"Of course," he nodded, "our investigation still entails locating Special Agent Alvarez."

"Is he being sought on murder charges now?" the reporter asked.

Murder? Michael felt the accusation like a blow.

"We have no comment on that at this time."

"But Special Agent Alvarez is being sought in connection with a case that involved the bank where Hector Ramos worked."

"Our office will make any new development available to the press as the situation warrants. Thank you." Buddy walked out of the picture, leaving the reporter to turn back toward the camera.

"To recap this breaking story, Special Agent Michael Alvarez is being sought in connection with embezzlement at a major local Miami bank. He has been missing since he disappeared from the hospital where he was recuperating from gunshot wounds. This station has been able to verify that Alvarez was working undercover at the bank and that Hector Ramos, the bank manager found murdered this morning, was a prime suspect in the case. At this time, the FBI refuses to comment on whether or not Alvarez is now being sought on suspicion of murder."

Michael looked across the table at Blair.

She turned her attention to him. "How can they

think these things about you?"

Before he could muster an answer, she continued. "Did you try to explain the situation to anybody?"

Michael couldn't tell her who he'd tried to explain things to. "Yes, I did."

"And?"

"Let's say it didn't work."

Her eyes flashed understanding. "Drew. You tried to tell Drew."

"I'll have to arrange my transportation." He stood.

"Don't do this, Michael. At the very least, you owe me enough information so I can understand why Drew would think for a single minute that you had anything to do with this." Anger colored her cheeks.

He said nothing. Couldn't.

That took the anger out of her expression. In its place came disbelief. "You think I believe this garbage?" Her voice rose. "You think I'd help you, make love with you, if I believed you capable of such a thing?" Her words cut across the sounds of the television.

"You slept with me six years ago. Who I am, what I am, made no difference until the end."

"What are you saying?"

Anger brought too-quick words to his mouth. "Six years ago you couldn't wait to get rid of me after spending a week doing little else but—" Michael bit off the crudity. He wouldn't let the years-old pain erase good sense.

In the stretching silence, Blair's eyes darkened. She started to say something, but Michael cut her off.

He couldn't handle any more. "You should have left me at Alice's."

"I couldn't do that again."

"Didn't you hear what Buddy said? Or rather, what he didn't say? They think I'm a thief and a murderer.

Your brother didn't find it far-fetched that a man of my position in life would steal money. That I'd dishonor the oath I took when I joined the agency."

"Then my brother is a fool."

"Don't you see, Blair? Nothing's changed. I'm still the man your family would have been shocked to see you bring home. Someone who doesn't fit in places like this." He swept his arm around, indicating their rich surroundings. "In the Davenport life."

Blair stared at him. "You think—"

"I stand accused not only of being a renegade agent and a murderer, but of stealing. Money, Blair." He stood. "That commodity that a Davenport doesn't even think of."

"You're right about one thing. You're still the same man. Closed, secretive. In my case, too aware of things that don't matter. You wouldn't do this. I don't know what happened. I don't know why Drew believes as he does, but it's not true."

Shaking his head, Michael crouched down before her. "*Niña*, why did you say no before?"

"Because I was afraid."

He wanted to understand. "Explain that to me."

"I was afraid of what you wouldn't tell me," she whispered. "I know it was about David now, but then—" Her eyes darkened to a deep, sea green. "I couldn't give up the silly dream of a nice normal marriage. A couple in a house surrounded by a white picket fence." Tears rolled down her cheeks. "Of a nine-to-five existence you couldn't live with. Of how boring you'd find me."

"Not because I'm an Alvarez and you're a Davenport?"

She shook her head.

"I'm a poor man by comparison, Blair."

141

"It was never about that." Her quiet words were like a blow.

"Jesus, Blair!" He closed his eyes briefly. "I was even more of a son of a—"

"I've thought about what we said that day. How you reacted, how I reacted. I just wanted to let it go, get it over with before I fell apart."

"How could you think I'd get bored with you?" He rested his hands on her thighs. "I almost killed myself making love to you that week. I couldn't keep my hands off you."

"Don't you see? Everything we did was intense, supercharged. We were squeezing a lifetime into seven days. It could never be the same."

He looked at her. "What was yesterday? What was last night?"

"As incredible as before. Better. But that's not what I'm talking about. We made love in the same supercharged environment that we went flying in. The same way you took me in the catamaran. It was a time impossible to repeat. Real life isn't like that."

"And you thought because I took you flying, took you sailing, I'd find you boring?" Incredulity made his voice rise. "Blair, I was trying to be a gentleman. If we hadn't been doing that, I'd have had you in bed the entire seven days."

"We couldn't have spent a lifetime making love either."

"When you said no, I thought that's all it was."

"It was too much. It scared me because I knew it wouldn't be easy."

"Easy?"

"You know, like that old song about love being as comfortable as an easy chair."

He looked into her eyes and knew easy would never

describe the years that followed their meeting. Even though he'd missed her with every fiber of his being, he was thankful she hadn't been with him.

"I didn't think about pregnancy because I was so overwhelmed," she said in a hushed voice.

"I thought about it for months. Hell, Blair, we didn't use a thing, ever. I'm still surprised—"

"I cried when I found out I wasn't." Her quiet words washed over him, soothing away years of hurt. "It was like losing you again. Until then there was hope that I'd have the courage to say yes. That I'd see you again."

Silence, thick and heavy, lay around them. Michael wanted to curse at the monumental misunderstandings, at the man he'd been. "I should have told you about David, about my assignment, Blair."

"I should have been mature enough to understand you couldn't."

He took a deep breath. "It wasn't the Bureau that kept me from telling you. It was me. I couldn't say it out loud yet."

She said nothing for long moments, then, "You did your job then. You'll get whoever has done this now."

Then she'd learn the truth.

That Drew was behind everything that had happened.

* * *

Blair woke with the midday sun shining brightly into the bedroom. She lay naked between sheets that smelled of Michael. She thought about the horrible mistakes they'd made before, remembered the person she had been then. She couldn't face losing Michael again and again as he went off in pursuit of what he loved to do. He wouldn't have been able to understand how important his mere presence was to her. How dependent she'd become in seven days.

143

Michael's voice drifted in to her from the living room. Curious she jumped out of bed and grabbed his T-shirt, throwing it on quickly.

"Okay," he was saying into the phone, "thanks, man." He hung up.

"Who was that?"

"Someone who's gotten us ID's so we can catch flights out this afternoon."

His words sliced into her. This was the blow she knew would come. But the hurt of it surprised her. "When will I see you again?"

"Blair, we can't—"

She turned away, not wanting him to see her pain.

"I have to clear my name. Any way I can." He sounded resigned, tired.

"I want to help." She didn't turn around. He would see her offer for what it was. Pleading.

"You can't."

With a deep breath, she mustered her strength and faced him. "I could talk to Drew, find out why—"

"No!" His emphatic response brooked no argument.

"Drew would listen—"

"Stay out of it, Blair. I'll deal with Drew."

"But he might—"

"We need to pack." He turned away, his stance tense.

Blair stared at his back, at the sleek skin covering smooth muscle. His jeans rode low on his hips and his feet were bare. She suddenly knew she'd been a fool. He was holding something back. Again. Loving him was a terrible mistake.

She walked back to the bedroom.

* * *

Michael turned in time to watch her leave. His shirt covered her to mid-thigh, but imprinted on his memory, forever, was the look of her. Courage and spirit.

Brimming with life, a little shy, a little wary, trusting in him.

He had the mindless urge to drive his fist into the wall. If he'd thought it would help, he would. But there was no help for it. Either he went down, or Drew Davenport did. Either way, Blair was impossibly out of reach.

* * *

The afternoon sun burned bright and hot as Blair drove out of the neighborhood on the way to the airport. Beside her, tense and quiet, sat Michael. He'd called Elena and spoken with her for a few minutes. In Spanish. He'd exchanged no more than a few words with Blair as they packed clean and dirty clothes into small suit cases. The cases would be checked so as not to draw attention from security.

All Blair had wanted to do was shut out reality, shut off tomorrow. The only thing that kept her sane was the fact that Michael was alive. That she had done something to help him.

"Make a right up here." Michael's voice broke into her thoughts.

"But that's not—"

"Turn right. Now."

Blair took only a second to do as she was told, her heart pounding. As soon as she straightened the wheel she glanced at Michael. He was staring into his side view mirror.

"Go two blocks and make another right. Don't use your blinker, don't touch the brake."

Blair took a quick look in the rear view mirror. A dark car followed about three car-lengths back. "Are they following us?" She hated the quiver in her voice.

"Get ready..." They approached the corner. "Turn." Michael's order was calm, cool, but Blair felt the urgency behind the quietly spoken words.

A quick glance in the rearview mirror answered her question. "They're following us."

Michael opened the glove compartment and pulled out a city map.

"We're crossing 14th," Blair said.

Tracing his finger across the map, he said, "Got it."

Blair looked back. The car loomed like a giant menace behind them.

"There's a split in the road. Up ahead. Stay to the left. We'll count three blocks and make a right."

Blair felt a trickle of sweat run down her back. The split was upon them too fast.

"On the third right." Michael counted, "One, two … here."

The quick turn forced her against the car door.

"Good girl. Take the next left."

"There's a truck com—"

"Turn!"

She did. The oncoming driver honked and raised his finger at her. Then she heard more horns blaring.

"Step on it."

Shaking, Blair pressed her foot on the accelerator, her hands frozen to the steering wheel. Then she felt Michael next to her, pressing her against the door. She relinquished the wheel to him, turning sideways to give him more room. He swung to the left and Blair clung to the door handle. When she instinctively moved her foot to the brake, Michael took over the accelerator.

They made another turn, this one spun the car around, and they took off again, amid blaring horns. Too afraid to watch what lay ahead, Blair kept her gaze on Michael.

His brisk movements jostled her, as did the speeding car. But his expression, a combination of intense concentration and studied control, reassured her. This was Michael. He could handle this. He scanned ahead then glanced at the rear view mirror. They bumped over a railroad track. He slowed the car.

Blair looked behind them. They'd lost the other car.

Michael made a right into a convenience store. "Stay here."

He scooted across the seat and got out, slamming the door. Blair watched him step up to a pay phone and dig in his pocket. Moments later he walked back to the car and leaned down to talk to her through the window.

"How did you rent this car?"

"Elena got it for us."

"Hand me the papers."

He stayed on the phone longer this time, talking earnestly to someone. Then he used the directory, jotting notes on the car rental folder.

Blair's knees nearly buckled when she got out of the car. They were alive, not crushed in the mangled heap of a wrecked car. The midday heat choked her, but she inhaled, taking in the smell of gasoline and exhaust. Regaining control of her legs, she signaled Michael and made for the station's bathroom.

When she came out, Michael was walking toward her.

He looked like nothing had happened. She couldn't read his eyes, hidden behind sunglasses, but his walk was the same measured stride he always used, one that hid strength he could call on in a single second. The walk that made him who and what he was. Calm, controlled, but ready to take charge, as he had minutes ago.

"You okay?" he asked as he got closer.

"Fine," she said, but realized her voice had quivered. Her fingers did the same when she pushed her hair behind her ears.

"Let's get a soda. Sugar will help." He pulled her along and she followed, wishing she could collapse and hug herself close. Hug him close, if only for a moment.

Inside the station, Michael bought drinks from the vending machine. Blair wrapped her hands around the cold, frosty can and drank the fizzy, sweet soda, her eyes watering. "Who were they?"

"You're sure you weren't followed yesterday, when you went out?"

"As sure as I can be. If they'd seen me, wouldn't they have already tried to get to you?"

Michael nodded.

"What do we do now?"

"The car rental company has agreed to pick up this car from here."

Blair felt like a leaf tossed on a storm, pulled and pushed by the winds of fate. A rumble of thunder sounded in the distance. Heat shimmered from the hot asphalt. A yellow cab pulled up in front of the station.

"That's ours," Michael said, opening the door. Heat and humidity pulled at them.

"What about the keys?"

"I told the agent where I'd leave them. Come on."

"Where are we going?"

"Miami."

Chapter Eleven

A few hours later, Blair found herself inside a single engine Cessna, soaring over central Florida. Michael had claimed to be a world-class soccer player, desperate to get to West Palm Beach to join his team. Blair played the role of his American girlfriend. She spent the entire trip trying to look empty-headed and adoring. Michael simply was what he pretended, exchanging stories with the pilot.

They landed at the West Palm Beach International Airport at dusk, ahead of a storm that blew in from the Atlantic.

"Good luck, Miguel," the amiable pilot said. "Taxis are out front." He pointed toward the terminal.

"*Gracias*, George." Michael took Blair's hand and led her across the tarmac as fat raindrops began falling.

Once inside, Blair turned to Michael. She'd been disturbed by the shift in their roles. He no longer needed her; he was in charge. It brought home how little she knew about his work. "How do you do that?"

"What?"

"Pretend to be someone else."

He looked out of the terminal, rain slashing at the windows. "We all pretend at some point in our lives." His dark eyes caught and held hers. "We pretend to keep from offending, to please someone, to be able to live with ourselves, to get by. To get what we want. Countless reasons."

She took in his words, knowing she'd pretended her love for him was something she could live without in order to survive. But survival had been empty. "You're saying that our lives are acts, intended to deceive either ourselves or someone else."

"Aren't they?"

"Maybe in your line of work."

"In life, too, *niña*. You should know that."

"Oh, my God! Blair!"

The high-pitched voice came from Blair's right. She turned to see a woman in an understated blue business suit walking quickly toward her. Michael, standing beside Blair, stiffened.

"Mary Lou!" Blair didn't have to feign surprise. Of all the possible complications, running into an ex-college roommate took the cake.

Mary Lou, all a-bubble and overly fragrant with expensive perfume, touched her cheek to Blair's. "It's been years."

Pulling away, Blair said, "A few."

"Goodness, Blair. It's been what? Four years or more. Since you broke up with Jim." She stepped back. "What are you doing here?"

Blair clutched for some quick answer. "I just arrived."

"Me too! My chauffeur should be here by now, but this rain's slowed traffic, so the limo's stuck." Mary Lou turned speculative eyes on Michael. "Who's your friend?"

Remembering the fiasco with Evan before the hurricane, Blair bit her lip.

"Miguel Romero," Michael said with a smile.

"Miguel," Mary Lou replied, extending her hand to Michael. "How long have you known Blair?"

Blair didn't like the sly undertone in the question.

"Not very long," he replied, the slight Spanish accent of the soccer player he'd pretended to be more pronounced.

"Well, let's catch up. I'd love to get to know Miguel," Mary Lou said, casting a sideways glance at Michael.

I just bet you would.

"What are you doing now, Blair?"

"I teach school."

"How charming. I ran into your mother last year some time, but she was with her mother, so we didn't have time to chat."

Mary Lou wouldn't have lowered herself to exchange pleasantries with a mere secretary, which was what Blair's grandmother was. She hid a smile. Her mother didn't like Mary Lou, though she'd never said so. Beth Davenport had too much class for that.

"What about you, Mary Lou?"

"I've taken over Daddy's real estate interests down here. He's much too tied up in Richmond and Roanoke. We have the house down here, you know, and so many friends from our circle. You must come and visit." She turned her attention to Michael. "And bring your friend."

"That's kind of you, but we have to take care of some business," Blair said.

"What kind of business are you in, Miguel?"

"Soccer, with the Argentinean Estudiantes." His cool answer seemed so effortless.

"Oh?" Mary Lou's brows rose and she turned toward Blair. "I didn't know Blair was interested in sports."

"Miguel's a friend of the family."

"Ah." The single word was innocent enough, but Blair could see that the woman's interest ran deep. "You'll have to bring Miguel to the house, then. Any friend of the Davenports is a friend of ours."

"Such a generous offer, Miss—" Michael looked from Mary Lou to Blair.

"Oh, this is Mary Lou Plath."

"Of Plath, Myers and Goldman."

"You've heard of Daddy, then, Miguel."

"Most certainly. I am interested in American investments."

"Then you must visit even if Blair can't. Daddy would love to meet you. I could introduce you around."

Trying to unclench her teeth, Blair managed, "I'm sure Miguel will get in touch with you when he has time."

"Of course." Mary Lou glanced toward the windows. "Oh, look! It's stopped raining. Jason should be here in just a moment. Do you need a ride into town?"

"No, thank you, Miss Plath," Michael replied. "We have a car."

The front doors swung open and in walked a uniformed chauffeur. Tall, blond, handsome. Perfect.

"Jason!" Mary Lou signaled. "Over here."

Blair watched the man approach, watched Mary Lou look him over, the way she would any of her father's expensive race horses. A trophy.

Had Michael thought she'd seen him as some sort of trophy?

"Only my small bag, Jason." Mary Lou indicated her tasteful leather bag.

How Jason stood being drooled over, Blair couldn't understand.

"Well, I have to run. Keep in touch, Blair. And Miguel, do call. I would love to see you again."

Mary Lou walked away with a wave, Jason on her heels. Just as the door began to close, Jason turned and gave Blair a look calculated to smolder.

Astounded, Blair stared. "Did he——?"

"Yes. I think Jason is interested in a new keeper." Michael smiled, but it wasn't a friendly smile.

"That's——"

"The person he pretends to be to get what he wants. Just like she pretended to be a friend of yours, when her real interest lay——"

"In you."

* * *

For the umpteenth time in the last half hour, as they drove south on I-95 toward Miami, Michael wanted to kick himself. Only he deserved worse.

His pride and his anger had consigned Blair to the Mary Lou's of the world. Her comment about Mary Lou wanting him was what he'd believed of her. It shamed him.

The lights of the other cars, rushing past at over eighty miles an hour on the freeway, lit up the inside of the rental car. He shouldn't be thinking about the past. He used the need for concentration to push aside the knowledge that the past made no difference anyway. He'd never have Blair. It had nothing to do with a tragic misunderstanding. Drew's involvement in what happened ruled out any future.

"How do you know about Plath, Myers and Goldman?" she asked.

Through Drew. Drew's case, though it probably shouldn't have been if the Davenports knew the Plaths.

"I've run across the name. Investment bankers." Investment bankers who'd settled a five-million-dollar case out of court. Thanks to Drew's investigation.

Silence greeted his reply.

All around them traffic rushed by, lights flashing on the wet freeway. In the distance, lightning lit up the night sky.

"Where are we going?"

"I've got some friends who can put us up for the night. In the morning you'll catch a plane back home." Michael glanced sideways and saw Blair's profile.

She nodded.

"Why don't you get some rest? It'll be a while. You might as well nap."

When he next glanced her way, Blair was asleep.

No matter what Drew had done, Blair wasn't now, and never had been, anything like Mary Lou Plath.

* * *

Dozing as they drove south, Blair couldn't turn off her thoughts. She'd drifted through life up until she met Michael. She had known where she'd go to college, knew her role was to play hostess for the Davenports and marry the right man.

She'd gone home after the week with Michael, put on an elaborate dinner party for her father, and left the next day for her senior year of college. Feeling empty and heartbroken. Michael's words tripped across her mind until a week later when she knew there would be no reason to contact him. No child with dark eyes for her to love.

Then she got mad. How dare he think of her a spoiled rich girl! A week of boiling anger and regret gave way to the realization that he had a right to think of her in that way. Michael had a purpose, a calling. She had nothing but the routine of obligation. She'd played it safe, avoiding the choice of something as necessary as a college major.

The sight of a dark-eyed boy of three, walking through a shop, made her choice for her. Blair's father had told her there no future in teaching; she wouldn't make a quarter of what her share of the Davenport fortune brought in each year. Her mother and both grandmothers had simply asked her if she was sure.

Jim Andrews wanted her to quit teaching. He needed her to stay home, entertain his clients. After all, that was what she'd been brought up to do. Her father, already angry because Drew had failed to come in to the business, gave her a speech about duty. Blair tried again to reason with Jim. He smiled and patted her hand, telling her that if she had spare time, she could volunteer at a school.

She wasn't sure. It had been hard. Harder than anything she'd ever done. All her illusions of how the children would hang on her every word vanished during the first five minutes of her first, carefully prepared, student teaching experience.

After that, Blair saw teaching as a challenge. It still wasn't easy, but it was rewarding when she got it right. She learned from other teachers, found her own way, her own methods. And it still wasn't easy. But it was a challenge with a purpose. So much more fulfilling than the life she'd been born to.

She'd made her choice, her first real, life-altering choice. She'd broken off her engagement to Jim and moved to Emerald Bay. Eventually, after all the gossip died down, her father came around.

Michael drove through another thunderstorm just as they exited the freeway.

Blair spoke over the noise of the wipers. "Are your friends expecting me?"

"They're not expecting me."

A few minutes later, they pulled in to the driveway of a house surrounded by a white picket fence. The storm had moved on, leaving behind a light drizzle.

"Wouldn't it be better to go to a hotel?"

"I'd rather not be so predictable."

"Do you think we were followed here?"

"Not to this house, no. But they'll know I'm in Miami. They know this is where I'd come."

"Who?"

"What do you mean who?"

"Who are 'they'? I know the FBI is after you. Drew, to be specific. But Hector Ramos is dead. Who are Eddie and his friend? Who else could be involved?"

Michael shut off the engine. The startling quiet brought goose bumps to Blair's arms.

"Somebody with an interest. Somebody who can hire help."

"Could it be someone from the bank? An accomplice of Hector's?"

Michael stared straight ahead, at the house, then back at Blair. "It's possible. Anything's possible."

"Someone's looking through the front window," Blair said.

He reached for the door handle. "I hope they still believe I'm one of the good guys."

Blair knew how much such an admission cost Michael. "You are one of the good guys." She doubted Michael had heard her, since he was already out of the car when she said it.

A plump, round woman, maybe fifty years old, opened the door and came running out. "Michael!"

"Selma *¿cómo estás?*" Michael hugged the little woman, lifting her off her feet.

"*Bien, hijo.*" She stepped back when Michael put her down and reached up to grasp his face between her hands. "You are not taking care of yourself."

"I'm fine, Selma."

"I will feed you. You need *frijoles negros* and *bistek.*" She patted his cheek, then turned toward Blair.

"You bring a friend, *hijo.*"

"This is Blair." Michael said. "She's helping me."

Selma looked from Blair to Michael and back. "Helping?" she echoed, then paused. "Oh. The trouble. *Claro*. But how can these people be *tan estúpidos*?" Selma shook her head. "*Dios mío ¿qué pasa con el mundo?* Come, Blair. Any friend of Michael is welcome in our home."

Michael held his hand out to Blair and she took it.

A fact not wasted on Selma, whose dark eyes flashed a smile.

"Come in, come in. We will eat soon, no? Go talk to Chabuca and Jimmy, Michael."

Blair took in the sight of the formal but worn furniture in the living room and the terrazzo floors polished to a high gloss. Wonderful food smells floated in through a swinging door she guessed led to the kitchen. A huge dining room table lay set, covered in a beautiful, though old, crocheted table cloth. Through a half-closed door off the living room, Blair could hear the sounds of the television. Michael stopped and bent close. "Let me do the talking."

"Famous last words," Blair murmured.

She saw Michael smile, his eyes bright and amused. "I won't tell them anything you can't keep up with."

The moment Michael pushed the door open, a stunning dark-haired girl bounced off a well-used couch and threw herself at him, holding on so tight Blair wondered how he could breath.

"Michael! Why didn't you tell me you were coming!" The girl, perhaps sixteen, pulled away and held one of his hands. She pulled down the legs of her too short shorts, then ran her fingers through long thick hair in a move calculated to be seductive.

"I didn't know I was coming, Chabuca," Michael replied, smiling and trying to disentangle himself from the girl.

Chabuca pouted, straightening the blouse she wore in an apparent attempt to draw Michael's attention to her chest.

"Jimmy, how's it going?" Michael looked around Chabuca at the handsome man standing behind her. Chabuca relinquished her hold.

"Great, Michael. I'm leaving in a week." Jimmy hugged Michael, then indicated they should sit.

Chabuca pulled Michael down beside her on the couch. "Is she your girlfriend?"

"This is Blair," he replied and, to Blair's amusement, tried to scoot away from the girl. Blair felt the compulsion to squeeze between them.

"Chabuca, leave him alone." Jimmy glared. "He's too old for you."

"Papi is fifteen years older than Mami." Chabuca crossed her arms over her voluptuous chest and, mouth set, flopped back against the couch, and turned her attention to the soccer match on television.

Jimmy rolled his eyes and shook his head.

"I heard you got the job," Michael said.

"Yeah. Couldn't believe it. My mother is wringing her hands, but my father is strutting like a rooster."

Michael laughed. "I bet he's proud. Your mother will come around."

"Did yours?"

"It took a while, but, yes. Now, well…"

"Your mother will have her vindication." Jimmy leaned forward, hands together between his knees. "What can I do?"

"Nothing."

"Come on, Michael! I know this town. I can help."

"Not without risk to your new job. If I'd known you were here I wouldn't have come."

"Don't be ridiculous. I can still be anyone I want to

be. You need it, I can get it."

Blair couldn't stop herself any longer. "What do you do, Jimmy?"

"I was with the local police. I just got a job with the State Department. I'm in Diplomatic Security."

"Helping me could land you in a heap of trouble."

A smile cut across Jimmy's face. "I'm good, man. Nobody better."

"Then let's keep you that way, okay?"

* * *

Somehow, Michael managed not to strangle young Chabuca. Some poor guy was going to have to deal with her when she worked the kinks out of her siren routine. He could see how uncomfortable Selma was, how Blair watched the girl, not sure whether to be amused or jealous.

"Michael, how long will you stay?" Selma asked as she cleared the table with Blair's help.

"We'll leave tomorrow early. Blair has a flight to catch."

"Blair is leaving?" Chabuca's best breathy voice drew everyone's attention.

Selma glared at her daughter.

"Michael is leaving, too," Jimmy interjected.

"I will bring sheets and blankets for you. One of you can sleep in John's big chair, the other on the couch." Selma patted Michael's shoulder.

"But, Mami, Michael can sleep in my room." At her mother's and brother's gasp, Chabuca hurried to add, "I have twin beds, Mami. He's too tall for the couch."

"Then I'll sleep on the chair." Michael hoped that would end the uncomfortable ordeal.

Chabuca flounced from the dining room.

Blair's lips quivered with suppressed laughter. She patted him on the shoulder, too, before taking a serving bowl into the kitchen.

Michael caught her hand and stopped her. "I'm going out for little while."

She froze at his words.

"I'll be back before you can miss me."

She nodded, her eyes locked to his. He wanted to reassure her, tell her everything would be okay.

"Be careful." She said the words so quietly, with so much meaning, he had to force himself to stay in his seat or he'd pull her in to his arms and crush her to himself.

He nodded and she walked into the kitchen.

"Telephone?" Jimmy asked into the silence.

"Yeah."

"There's one outside the old bodega."

Michael pulled out of the driveway, knowing he didn't want to contact anyone. But he had no choice. Blair had to get a plane back and she couldn't do it as herself. It wouldn't do for her to be caught helping him. She would be in danger because she could prove he didn't kill Hector Ramos. A quickly placed phone call would get her fake documentation and a plane ticket.

* * *

She was asleep when Michael got back, curled up on the couch, a light blanket covering her. When he walked down the hall to the bathroom, Jimmy came out of his room.

"Go okay?"

"Yeah." As okay as he could hope.

Jimmy nodded.

"This shouldn't touch you."

"You haven't done anything wrong."

Michael couldn't help it. He looked back into the den where Blair slept. She was what he'd done wrong.

At Michael's silence, Jimmy continued. "Don't blow

it, Michael. She's worth the fight."

"The fight's hopeless. Either way it goes, she gets burned."

Jimmy paused, his hand on the door handle. "You'll take care of it. I'm here if you need me." Then he quietly closed his door, leaving Michael to wonder if he really could take care of it.

Minutes later, after a quick shower, he walked back into the living room. Blair was awake, sitting on the couch, the blanket tossed aside. "Where did you go?"

"I've arranged for another ID and a plane ticket for you."

She plucked at the blanket, looking down. "I'd rather stay." She didn't look up.

The sight of her, head bent, her hair a curtain around her face, made Michael's heart ache. He squatted down before her. She still didn't look up. "It can't be, *niña*. Things are in too big a mess."

She lifted her head, her eyes even with his. "We could try."

He pushed her hair behind her ears and let his hands rest on her shoulders. "Now's not the time." He struggled for words to explain without explaining. He hadn't noticed that his thumbs were gently rubbing circles on her collarbones. He stopped when he did.

"I was afraid." Blair's eyes shone gold. "Before, more than this time." With one hand she touched his stomach, where he'd been cut. "I should be more scared now, but I know you can fix this. You will make it right again."

Michael shivered at her soft caress. He would get Drew Davenport. And damn himself to a life without her because of it.

"When it's over, I'll be waiting." That gentle hand skimmed across his chest to his face. She used her fingers to trace his lips.

To love me or curse me? The question burned through him, but her hands seduced him in to planting a soft kiss in her palm, their eyes locked together.

Her eyes blazed hot, her breath caught. Michael saw the flare of passion and groaned. "We can't. Not here."

"I know." She ran one hand down his chest. When he closed his eyes to her touch, she added. "Chabuca might walk in and find me touching what's hers."

Through helpless shivers of desire, Michael laughed. But common sense prevailed. He pulled her hand away, wishing he could love Blair one last time. One time to hold him. "Sleep with me, Blair. I want to feel you against me."

They accommodated themselves on the couch, back to front, adjusting their bodies for maximum comfort. Blair wiggled against him, her behind in his lap. And Michael wished they were somewhere else, some place that would give him the freedom to love her again.

* * *

Blair woke with a crick in her neck. The only pleasant sensation was the feel of Michael, his body solid and radiating heat, behind her. She blinked at the dim light of early dawn and tried to move her head to adjust her position. Michael tightened his arm, which lay relaxed and heavy across her ribs, and pressed his hand against her stomach.

"Don't move." The soft rumble of his voice sent shivers up her spine. His exploring hand sent shivers to other parts of her body. "I need a cold shower."

"Mmhm." Blair scooted closer.

She felt his hand cup her breast, his beard roughened cheek rubbing against the back of her neck.

"Get up, Blair, before I do something we'll both regret."

She rolled her head to one side, wincing at sore muscles, and sat up.

"Sit on the floor. I'll rub your neck."

That was how Selma found them. Blair, with her head forward, eyes closed, reveling in the feel of Michael's fingers working the kinks from her abused muscles.

"*Buenos días*," the older woman said, smiling.

Blair thanked heaven she hadn't pushed Michael harder, tempted him more.

"Did you sleep well?"

"Very well, thank you." Blair put her hand over Michael's to still his movements.

"But that old couch hurt your back. I am sorry." Selma winked, to Blair's amusement. Did the older woman think more had gone on in her homey den?

Michael cleared his throat and stood. "I'm going to shower. We need to get to the airport by eight." He stepped over Blair and made his way up the hall.

Blair watched him walk away, wondering what she would do while she waited for him to come back to her.

"Michael's father is a friend of my husband," Selma said when the bathroom door shut. "I have known them since they came to America when Michael was fifteen." She touched Blair's arm lightly. "He is a good boy. You know your heart *¿no?*"

Before Blair could answer, Selma nodded, turned, and walked away.

* * *

Michael watched for the intersection where he would meet Manuel Gomez. Beside him, Blair took in the sights of the Cuban business district, already busy with people walking up and down the street. He wondered what she thought of this place, so foreign to her, not only in language and culture, but also so different from her heritage in Virginia society.

He found a parking spot on the street and finally caught sight of his informant. Manuel was Colombian. He had worked for Michael in exchange for leniency for some petty crimes and had proven loyal because Michael made an effort to treat him fairly. Other agents, both the Anglos and those of Cuban descent, tended to lord it over the scrawny Colombian, acting as if they were doing the man a favor by using him. Michael knew human nature well enough to know he'd do better without that attitude.

That attitude. He had immediately jumped to the conclusion that Blair wouldn't marry him because he wasn't rich and he was Latino. Now he saw it as some remnant of the boy he'd been, thrust into a place where heritage defined so much of a person. It was what made him treat the Manuels of the world with more fairness than they often deserved.

It had also made him a sitting duck for Drew Davenport.

* * *

Blair thought about Selma's question as she watched Michael get out of the car to talk to a really disreputable looking man. Yes, she knew her heart, but she wasn't sure what it meant to give her heart to Michael.

All around the parked car, predominantly Spanish language signs advertised American products. Rolling down the window, Blair heard nothing but Spanish spoken on the street. Spanish she couldn't keep up with, having taken only three years of the language in high school.

As Michael turned his back to the car and spoke earnestly to the scruffy looking man, Blair understood her feelings, clearly, for the first time. She trusted Michael. She believed in him. She loved him. But she'd spent very little time with him. Yes, she had been frightened of giving up her dreams, but she'd also been afraid of her ability to cope should anything happen to him. And behind those two fears loomed an ugly truth.

She'd also been afraid of this—this difference in them. It made her feel small because the differences were what Michael thought had made her say no. Only he thought it was snobbishness on her part. Her wealth and social standing in contrast to his life.

Becoming a teacher and living within that income didn't erase the differences between herself and Michael. The cultural differences were nothing. Yes, he had an entryway into a culture foreign to her, ease with a language she didn't understand.

His need for excitement was what really set them apart. No, this wasn't the type of excitement he loved. But the truth was there: he would never want a job devoid of risks.

Michael turned from the stranger, looked up and down the street, and walked back to the car.

"Here's your new ID. Your ticket's waiting for you at the ticket counter. You'll be home by this afternoon."

Blair blinked back a rush of tears. She didn't want to go home. She wanted to stay here and help.

But with no skills or knowledge to contribute, she could do nothing but make it harder for him.

* * *

They parked the car in the short-term parking lot and walked into the terminal, the morning heat already building. Inside the crowded airport, they found the ticket counter and lined up to check her in.

"Shouldn't you leave now?" It was the last thing in the world she wanted, but it wasn't safe for him.

"I should be okay until you're ready to go through security." Michael wore dark sunglasses and a Marlins cap, backwards.

"What are you going to do?"

Behind the glasses, Blair could make out the fact that Michael was studying the faces of anyone who looked like a security officer. "I'm going to clear my name."

His certainty made her smile. And gave her hope. "I'll be waiting."

He turned his gaze toward her.

She didn't like his silence, the wary stillness of his body.

They approached the counter in silence and checked the single bag he'd forced her to bring. Then they made their way toward the concourse from which her plane would take off. Michael stopped as they approached the metal detectors.

"I don't think it would be a good idea for me to get any closer to security."

She turned quickly. "You've got a gun?" Dumb question. Of course he had a gun. "You'll get to the bottom of this mess, I know you will."

"I sure as hell plan to try." He looked toward the security officers manning the metal detectors. "Thanks, Blair."

When she looked surprised, he continued. "For taking care of me during my recuperation." His eyes shone with teasing humor. "My stamina hasn't been what it should be."

"Oh, you did all right." Blair felt a flush of heat on her cheeks at how her words had sounded.

He smiled, a devilish smile on his lips. "Yeah, well, I hope you were satis—"

"Don't!" She clapped her hand over his mouth, looking around. "Someone might hear you."

"And who would know what I'm talking about?" he asked around her hand.

The movement sent jittery pleasure down her arm. She moved back. "I should go."

"Take care of yourself."

"You, too." Drumming up her courage, she reached out and touched his chest. "When will I hear from you?"

He looked down at her, his dark eyes hidden behind the glasses, his angular features tight. "You'll hear." Then he bent and kissed her, one quick, hard kiss, his hands gripping her upper arms.

Blair wanted to get closer, to feel his arms around her, to have him gentle the kiss, but Michael held her away.

"You'll understand then." With that, he turned and walked away.

Chapter Twelve

She'd understand what? Blair stared after Michael. That he had no intention of contacting her?

That she wouldn't see him again?

That it was really over?

She nearly stumbled as she made her way to join the end of the line for security. She spun around, searching for him in the crowd. But he was gone. Just as surely as he'd vanished from her life six years ago. She'd been twice the fool this time, because she'd grown to harbor the hope that they had a chance, secretly believing that this time around, they'd make it.

She wouldn't cry. She'd done that before and it hadn't made her feel any better, hadn't made any difference. The only thing that had made any difference was finally taking control of her own life.

Well, she'd done that. The wreck she'd made of her relationship with Michael six years ago had resulted in Blair Davenport becoming who she was today.

To quote Scarlett O'Hara: tomorrow was another day. She'd deal with it all then. Because it wasn't over between her and Michael. She wouldn't let it be.

Once through security, her mind still whirling with a mixture of hurt, confusion and determination, she walked down to her gate, at the very end of the concourse. There she sat in numb silence until she realized she'd better go to the bathroom before she boarded.

Coming out of the bathroom, she saw him. An FBI agent. He had to be, dressed as he was in a suit, red and blue tie, and white shirt. He scanned the crowd, searching, looking. For Michael.

No, she was being paranoid. No one knew Michael would be here.

But just in case, Blair swung her backpack onto her back and walked into a bookstore. Moments later, a University of Miami baseball cap on her head, she tiptoed to look out and search for the agent. A jolt of alarm ran up her back. Drew had joined the agent. Soon, two more agents joined them.

Torn between staying out of sight and a burning need to warn Michael, Blair hid behind a tall magazine stand. She could try to get to a phone and call Selma's to see if she could contact him.

She sneaked another look at the gate area. Drew was talking, pointing as if to direct two of the men to search another area. They fanned out, except for Drew and the first agent. They moved toward the check-in counter. Blair searched the crowd for the other two agents. They'd each gone in opposite directions, searching the nearby stores.

The first call for her flight came over the speakers. Drew nodded at something the other man said, spoke to one of the flight attendants, still checking in passengers, then picked up the telephone behind the counter. The other agent, a short blond, entered the jet-way leading down to the plane.

Blair walked quickly toward a bank of telephones situated away from the check-in counter. Positioning herself to lean well in toward the phone, she opened the phone book, only to close it in frustration at the number of Sanchezes listed. She couldn't call Selma. Besides, Michael didn't seem to be going back there. He had brought his few things with him in the car.

Trying not to panic, she walked away from the phones. She'd go back to the main terminal. She couldn't afford to be found here. Drew would know she'd been with Michael. She wouldn't allow that to happen.

She wanted to run, to get away from what was a dead end, Gate 60 at the end of the concourse, but a quick glance over her shoulder told her that Drew and one agent had fanned out and were looking in each store along the concourse, Drew on one side, the other agent on the other.

A golf cart carrying those passengers unable to make the walk down the concourse came toward her, ringing its bell. She moved behind it, hoping Drew wouldn't see her, and set off walking at what she hoped was an unhurried pace.

At Gate 30, she entered a coffee shop and glanced back.

Drew and the agent were still searching, shop to shop. They scanned each gate area, then moved on. The blond agent she'd seen go down the jet-way now walked straight down the center of the concourse. If she didn't move quickly, they'd find her.

Three pilots, tall men, walked toward the terminal. She positioned herself directly in front of them, careful to move at their same leisurely pace as they exchanged what sounded like wild stories about a party they'd attended.

Finally, she passed the security area and turned toward the exit to short term parking. But Michael had probably already left. She'd have to wait it out. The bathroom seemed like a good place.

She stepped into a stall, but was too nervous to stay. Again back in the main terminal, she walked into a bookstore and stood behind a heavyset woman who perused some recent magazines. She leaned to one side to look over the woman's shoulder into the terminal, scanning for Drew and his agent.

"What the hell are you doing?" The whispered words from next to her nearly made her jump.

Startled breathless, Blair turned and saw Michael, back turned toward the terminal, his dark eyes furious.

"Drew's here, with other agents."

"I know," he bit out, glancing toward the terminal.

Blair felt him stiffen. The blond agent came into view.

"I'll be damned," he said quietly.

"Do you know him?"

The last call for her flight came over the speaker. Drew came into view and he and the blond agent moved to stand in front of security, each facing a different way. Blair felt the ridiculous urge to giggle, to yell and tell them they were right under their noses.

Long minutes later, after the final call for her flight, the two other agents joined Drew and the blond agent. Michael wandered slowly toward the cash register, his head bent.

Blair watched him, then glanced toward the terminal. Drew and the agents spoke, then each walked quickly in different directions. Drew headed toward the main entrance.

"Go to the ladies' room," Michael said when he walked back to her.

"I'd rather stay with you."

"Damn it, Blair. Go and stay there until I get you."

"But—"

"Go! And don't go looking for Drew."

Michael took off behind the blond agent. Blair watched him, itching to go after Drew and explain what a mistake he'd made.

* * *

Michael blessed his decision to wait until he knew Blair's plane had taken off. If he hadn't, he wouldn't have known that James Meyer had led Drew here.

James, who also used Manuel, must have gotten word from the Colombian and given away his location to Drew. James owed him a big favor because of a case the younger agent had screwed up, so Michael had asked him to look into the Hector Ramos case when he'd first found that Hector was skimming more than the usual amounts. James had an accounting degree, and while Michael had been trained for the bank job, a second look never hurt. While he didn't expect James to be derelict in his duty, he was still surprised he'd led Drew here.

That didn't mean that Drew wasn't responsible for setting him up. It did prove Michael wasn't a very good judge of character. He hadn't thought Manuel would contact James, nor that James would give him up.

The crowded airport provided plenty of cover for Michael, but also for James and Drew. Michael reached the security area for another concourse and didn't see them. Doubling back, he checked the stores and snack bars, carefully keeping an eye out for any agents. Then he heard excited talking, some yelling, and saw people milling about the area around the bathroom where he'd left Blair.

Forgetting caution, he ran down and pushed through the crowd gathered in front of the women's bathroom. Security officers were trying to hold back onlookers, but Michael managed to get through in the confusion. At the entrance to the bathroom, he asked a woman what had happened.

"A man in a suit came in here and shot at a pretty

young woman."

Cold fear calmed Michael. "Where is she?"

"Oh, she ran. Good for her, I say. I just hope he doesn't catch her. Where are the police?"

Michael put one hand on the woman's shoulder and pushed her aside.

"Hey, you can't go in there. It's the women's—"

Trying to remain composed, Michael looked around the bathroom. Wide-eyed women, some holding children by the hand, stood frozen in place, staring back at him. No one was in any of the stalls. One of the sinks had a hole in it. The impact of the bullet had cracked the porcelain. Another bullet had struck the mirror above, shattering it.

"I told you, Mister, she ran," the woman who'd spoken to him said from behind.

"Which way?"

"I didn't see."

Where would she go? What would she do?

Drew couldn't have anything to do with this. He wouldn't hurt his sister.

Michael jogged through those gathered around, passersby too caught up with watching the confusion to take any notice of him. Standing in the busy terminal, Michael looked both ways. How could he find her? Would she go to security?

Scanning the crowd, he found a group of three airport security officers standing next to a bank of phones. He walked to the phones and tried to listen to what they were saying.

"Man, that FBI agent was pissed. He was saying that this woman was with a guy they've been chasing for over a month. Says the guy—remember that agent they've been looking for?—tried to kill her to cover up something. They're after him big time."

"What about the woman?"

"Would you believe she's the sister of another Fed?"

"Shit, that's a mess I'm glad we're clear of."

Michael hadn't seen Eddie and company. Maybe they had a different crew in Miami. It didn't matter who had done this. It only mattered that they had.

Where are you, Blair?

Cold sweat trickled down Michael's back. In a moment of stark panic, he wanted to run up and down the terminal yelling her name. Then sanity took over.

Where would she go?

Back to me.

He sprinted toward the door that led to the short term parking lot, trying to concentrate, picturing, over and over, where he'd parked. Pulling his Glock and keeping it down at his side, he slowed, alert, looking for any sign of danger.

Fear, heat and humidity plastered his shirt to his back. He wiped his forehead with his arm. Concentrated calm made him approach each support beam as if it were the one place where the shooter was hiding. Waiting.

As he got closer to the car, Michael began to have doubts. What if she'd run to Drew? She might be safe if she made it to him, but if she didn't... If something had—

He wouldn't think that. He would find her. Even if he had to risk running into Drew.

His rental car sat among the other cars in the lot, just as he'd left it. Mouth dry, Michael looked around the area. No one in sight. Pulling the pistol up, he approached the final beam.

Nothing.

Circling from the outside, well away from the rental, his eyes always checking, he moved around, circling his car.

Crouching down, he checked beneath the cars.

Nothing.

Where are you, Blair?

A bank of elevators lay to the right. He and Blair had taken one of those down. He'd run up the three flights of stairs this time, knowing not to risk entrapment in an elevator. But Blair didn't have his survival skills. She wouldn't know to avoid the elevators.

He fought off the fear. Fear would cloud his judgment.

The elevator door swung open and a couple stepped out. Michael lowered the Glock and kept walking around. His car lay to his left now. One final support beam stood in his way.

Pistol at the ready by his side, he approached. Scanning the area around his car, he saw a movement so small and so quick he wondered if he had seen it. No one lurked behind the support beam. Michael concentrated his attention on the cars parked around his. Something had moved.

There.

The pickup truck two spaces down from his rental. He crouched, looking beneath the truck.

Nothing.

A trickle of sweat rolled down his temple. Michael moved quietly toward the truck, watching and listening for anything that might indicate that the shooter was near.

He passed his own car, carefully making his way toward the pickup. There was something in the back end. A tarp or some sort of drop cloth crumpled enough for something to be beneath it.

Raising his pistol, he jerked the tarp up.

Blair stared up at him with wide, panic-filled, green

eyes.

Michael looked all around before jumping up into the bed of the truck. Blair was silently sobbing, hugging her knees, lying on her left side, watching him.

"Blair, it's me."

She nodded, but kept her death-grip on her legs. The uncomprehending look in her eyes scared him.

"Let's go, Blair."

She took a ragged breath. "I can't move."

The sound of her voice, so broken, made his heart shatter. God, how frightened she must have been. He pushed his pistol into the back waistband of his jeans and knelt before her. With one hand, he smoothed her hair from her face. With the other, he wiped drying tears from her cheeks. "It's okay, I'm here."

"He shot at me, Michael. In the bathroom. There were children. Lots of them. There was this mother who— I ducked. He shot the sink." Choppy breaths punctuated her words. "Then the mirror. I was going to find Drew." She grabbed her knees tighter. "You told me not to, but—"

Surely Drew hadn't shot at her. Michael fought the reaction he felt coming. He rubbed her right arm, from shoulder to wrist.

"When I came out of the bathroom, that blond agent saw me. He didn't say anything. He just," she took a breath, "shot."

"James shot at you." Cold fury kept Michael's voice low.

"That's his name?"

Michael felt some of the tenseness leave her limbs. He continued rubbing, gently, trying to soothe her trembling. "Yes, that's his name."

She pressed her face into her knees. Michael looked around the lot again before touching her cheek. "We have to go now, Blair."

"Okay." She said the word with utter calmness, but she didn't move.

"I'll take care of you," he murmured with a silent prayer, bending to put an arm around her.

"I'm not brave, Michael." Her voice wobbled. "I was so scared. I wanted you there." She bit her lower lip. "And I didn't want you there. He's the one who wants to kill you, isn't he?"

"It's okay. He can't hurt you now."

She fought a sob. "What if he gets you?" Her words tumbled over his thoughts.

"He won't. We're going to be fine." He said it for Blair, to reassure her, but he wasn't so sure. James had set him up perfectly. Drew couldn't know that James had tried to kill Blair. No matter what else Drew might be, he wouldn't hurt his sister. This wasn't the time to worry about Drew or the whole damn mess. The most important thing was to get Blair out of the way, get her to safety.

He crouched in front of her, pulling her up, holding her in an awkward embrace, her knees against his chest, rubbing up and down her back. Her trembling stopped and Michael felt her muscles relax. "Let's go, *querida*."

Her knees shook when she finally stood, but she straightened her back and got out of the truck. Michael, tense and alert for danger, got her into the rental and drove out of the lot. No one followed. As they left the airport, Michael saw three cruisers, lights and sirens going, headed for the terminal.

"Buckle up," he told Blair, looking across the seat. She'd been terrified, but she'd shown more courage than anyone he'd ever met.

She fumbled with the seat belt. "Where are we going?"

"Someplace safe."

* * *

There could be no safe place, Blair thought. Michael hadn't seen that man's face. Smiling. Cold. Heartless. He'd not reacted to the screaming mothers, the sobbing children. His hard gray eyes had found her and, unflinching, he'd shot. She'd never know how or why she'd moved. But she had.

Now, at least, Michael knew who to look for. Who to hide from.

With conscious effort, she unclenched her fists. She ached all over.

Michael reassured her by his mere presence. They were on the Venetian Causeway, crossing Biscayne Bay, the sun hot behind them. Thunderclouds, huge and dark, loomed across the bright blue sky. The air conditioner blew its refrigerated air at her, cooling her sweat- soaked clothes, chilling her.

Once on Miami Beach, they turned north, the huge beach hotels towering to the right. The asphalt shimmered with heat waves. Blair wished she were outside, soaking in the warmth. She aimed the air conditioning vents away from herself. Michael turned down the blower.

When Blair realized where Michael was going, she hugged herself and bit back the shivers. "The Fontainebleau?"

"Hide in plain sight."

"We look like we've been running from murderers." For some reason her words struck her as funny. She giggled.

Michael pulled into the check-in lane, unbuckled his seatbelt, and turned toward her. With one strong hand, he cupped her cheek. "It's okay. We're safe."

"As safe as you were hiding when Nell blew in?" An

uncontrolled shudder shook her.

"I'm Miguel, the soccer player."

"I don't make a good bimbo," she said between clenched teeth.

Michael smiled and his hand slipped to the back of her neck. "No, you don't. You're smart and brave."

She tried to smile, but her face felt frozen.

"We don't have luggage because it didn't arrive on our flight from Buenos Aires and we're a mess because we had a flat on the way in. They'll understand." His voice, as well as his hands, soothed her shattered thinking.

"I don't know if I can walk into the lobby right now." She hated admitting such a weakness, but better to admit it now than to fall on her face once inside.

Michael's eyes softened. His hand on her neck gentled even more. He undid her seatbelt and pulled her closer, fitting her to him, adjusting their bodies so her head rested in the crook of his neck. He was sticky, sweaty. He'd been as scared as she. The knowledge made her pull back slightly. "I was so glad to see you."

"I know, *querida*, I know. I was glad to see you, too." His face descended to hers and he brushed a gentle kiss on her lips.

He felt so alive, so good, so very real. Blair was so thankful he hadn't been killed. That she hadn't been killed. She grasped his shirtfront and pulled him closer, her mouth seeking his for a deeper kiss. Michael obliged. He consumed her with passion, until she felt warm again.

Too quickly, he pulled away. His lips, so beautiful, tempted her to touch. Against her fingers, he spoke. "We need to go inside."

"Can we afford this?"

"Your practical streak," he smiled, nodding. "Yes,

but we can't stay long. What cash I have is nearly gone."

"I have my credit—"

He shook his head. "We can't afford to be traced."

"Oh." Of course. They'd been using cash all along.

With a quick, hard kiss, he pulled her out of the car, and, arm around her waist, led her into one of the most famous hotels on the beach.

He was good. The clerk practically fell at his feet trying to make up for the lost luggage and flat tire. They had absolutely nothing to carry upstairs, so the bellhop was dismissed, looking disappointed at missing the opportunity to take an international soccer player to his room.

Blair clung to Michael's hand all the way across the impressive lobby with its bowtie marble floor. They'd nearly reached the bank of elevators, when Blair felt her knees go rubbery. Michael quickly put his arm around her waist again.

"The elevator at the airport. I was so stupid, I took it. He could have been there. I didn't think—"

"It's okay," he soothed.

The bell chimed and one elevator opened, the passengers, all dressed in shorts, stepped out. Blair leaned on Michael, realizing her mistake. She hadn't thought beyond her need to get away and find Michael. Hadn't thought at all, really, until this moment when she realized just how vulnerable she had been. How vulnerable that made him. If she had died, Michael would never have known who had put him through the hell of the past weeks, who was trying to kill him.

Once inside the elevator, Michael pulled her into his arms. The solid beat of his heart made her burrow closer.

She wrapped her arms around him, loving his strength. She might never have seen him again.

Stretching a little on shaky legs, she tasted the skin of his throat, where his pulse beat so strongly. She could hear his breathing, a little fast, over the muffled blipping sound of the rising elevator.

"God, Blair," Michael said against her hair, pinning her to him.

She searched for his mouth, fear and relief mingling in a need so strong she couldn't tell if she still shook from reaction or from want.

Michael accepted her desperation. Holding the back of her head with one hand, her hip with the other, he devoured her mouth. Eyes closed, Blair felt the consuming hunger of his kiss, the roughness of his unshaven chin.

The elevator chimed and they jumped apart in time to see the elevator door swing open on their floor. The hall was empty. Michael's hot, dark eyes bored into hers. With a small sound of relief, she once again stepped into his arms.

Michael bent and kissed her again, his mouth open and hungry against her own. He crushed her to himself. "You're like a drug. I can't get enough."

She laughed, a jerky, jittery laugh, and kissed the spot where his neck met his shoulder.

They pulled apart, walking down the empty hallway, each step bringing them closer to privacy. With one hard, biting kiss, he stopped her as he fumbled the key card.

Once inside, the door shut firmly against the world, Michael pushed her against the wall as she tugged at his shirt, desperate to pull it off and feel the heat of his skin. When he raised his arms to rid himself of the offending garment, she ran her hands through the crisp hair of his chest. Looking up into his eyes, she saw him watching her, his face stark with need.

Blair grabbed at his shoulders, her mouth seeking and finding his. She felt his hands on her arms as he kissed her.

He released her, pulling her away from the wall, running his hands down to her hips, pulling her against him. The hunger of his mouth was matched by the thrust of his hips against her. He adjusted their bodies, rubbing the hardness of his arousal against the juncture at her thighs. Breaking the kiss, he pulled her T-shirt off and buried his face in her neck.

The room spun as he walked her backwards to the bed. His mouth sought and found her nipples through the cotton lace of her bra. The frenzied pull of his lips, the unrelenting hunger of his body, combined to make her sob with need and frustration.

Then she was falling, Michael atop her, as they tumbled to the bed. Blair opened her eyes to find him pulling down the bra to release her breasts. With fingers amazingly gentle for all the desperation of his movements so far, he caressed her, then bent and took a nipple into his mouth. Suckling, he undid the single button of her shorts and pulled down the zipper. Kneeling over her, his powerful body radiating heat, he pulled down the shorts and her panties, and pushed her knees up.

A wildness in his eyes made Blair choke back a cry. This was Michael uncontrolled. Waves of male intensity rolled off him as he jerked at his jeans. Desperate to help, Blair fought him for the zipper, her fingers feeling the hard outline of his erection.

They both sighed on ragged breaths when he took her, thrusting hard and deep.

Supporting himself above her with flexed arms, he stared down. "Blair," he said in a hoarse and desperate voice.

He withdrew, his eyes never leaving hers, then pushed back into her. Blair had never felt anything so potent. Her body open and wanting, welcomed his invasion; her heart, open to him, reveled in the reassurance of life.

With a rumble from deep in his chest, Michael blanketed her body, his thrusts attuned to a powerful rhythm that had Blair tilting her hips to keep him with her.

Emotions and sensations spiraled out of control. Michael increased the tempo of his thrusts until Blair felt only the hardness of his body so intimately joined with hers. The bubble of heat that rolled through her wrung gasps of surprise and pleasure from her.

Above her, Michael seemed to lose all finesse, and with one hard, deep thrust, joined her.

* * *

Michael pulled away from the heat of Blair's body. They were slick with sweat. He felt like he'd run ten miles. Beneath him, she lay still, her head turned to one side, her eyes closed.

He began remembering. Everything he'd done since he'd slammed the door behind them. He'd been a wild man, never giving her time, never letting her feel, simply taking over.

Fear had propelled him. She could have died. He could have lost her to a man, who for whatever reason, was determined to destroy him. With utmost care, he curved his body around hers, sliding one arm under her neck. She didn't move.

He'd hurt her once with words. Now his actions had almost gotten her killed.

With one hand, he pushed her hair away from her neck and watched her pulse beating. He loved her beyond reason, beyond good sense.

He had to get her away from him, had to find a way to make her safe.

Her eyes fluttered open and she turned back toward him.

He never expected to see her look at him like this. Never.

Trust, relief, satisfaction, love. All shone from the clear depths of her eyes.

And for that one instant, he felt blessed contentment.

Until responsibility took over.

No one, especially not him, would ever hurt her again. No matter what it took.

Chapter Thirteen

Michael was looking at her with something akin to fierceness. Reaching up, Blair smoothed one dark, arched brow with her fingertips.

"It's going to be okay, *niña*." He took her fingers and kissed them.

In that moment, she clearly saw, for the first time, what it was that made him who he was.

He was a protector. A man who believed in right, in justice, in guarding life. That was why he lived it so fully. It mattered to him. People mattered to him. It was why he'd gone into the army, why he'd joined the Bureau.

Selfish, she had been so damned selfish. She had wanted him in her fantasy of that house with a picket fence. A place where he could not be what he was born to be.

She felt a tear roll from one eye. Michael caught it, rubbing the drop between finger and thumb.

"I didn't mean to put you in danger, to hurt you, Blair."

She swallowed. "You didn't. That man did."

"What about when we got here? I wasn't exactly gentle."

He looked so contrite, so at odds with the man he'd been only seconds ago, that Blair smiled. "I didn't break."

"You wanted comfort, I—"

"You gave me comfort. I wanted you. Not a carefully planned seduction."

"Can't accuse me of that." Light was back in his eyes, but behind the easy words, Blair sensed something else, something he once again wasn't sharing with her.

She was afraid to ask what it was, afraid she'd lose her resolve not to let anything come between them. Especially as she lay here, so safe, in his arms.

She only had to get through one minute at a time. She could cope, she would move on to practicalities. That had always helped her.

"Why is this James doing this?" Blair couldn't control the shiver than ran down her body.

Michael pulled her closer, scooting her so she lay on her side facing him, legs tangled with his. With one hand, he rubbed her back gently. "He was trying to set me up. Make it look like I killed you."

The cold words were so at odds with his touch, that Blair grabbed his hand, pressing it hard against her chest. "But why?"

"The only explanation is that he's involved in the embezzlement. I helped him out a couple of years ago. He'd made a mistake that nearly ruined a case he was working. He said he owed me, so I asked him to double check a few things. Nothing illegal, just a second look. He's based in Atlanta but he's working a case that brings him to Miami pretty often."

"Why didn't you call Drew?"

Blair felt Michael's body tense. "Drew's been involved from the beginning. He's coordinating the investigation along with another related one. I wanted someone who hadn't seen the case as it progressed."

"So you asked this man for help." Blair turned that over in her mind. "Could he have sent Eddie and his friend after you?"

"It's possible. James may have been pulled into the investigation officially at some point. I wouldn't have known that, not after I was shot and in the hospital. Like Drew, he knew I had a friend on the island. I'm sure I probably mentioned that I'd gone there a few times. It was a good guess, luck on their part."

"What about at the motel?"

"My carelessness, or again, a lucky guess on their part, I don't know."

Blair thought back. "Who got us the IDs and plane tickets in Tampa?"

"An informer I have there," Michael said. "Informers are registered, so if Drew or James had any suspicions that I might be there, they would have contacted him."

"Eddie was the man who claimed to be an FBI agent. But Drew was at the airport today, with James and other agents."

Michael pulled her closer, nuzzling her neck. "I'm sure James told him. Drew knows you helped me. He knows you're in Miami. If James had killed you, it would have appeared that I had."

"Drew won't believe that. I'll talk to Drew. He'll understand."

Michael rolled away from her and stood. Suddenly cold and alone, she said. "Michael?"

Running his hands through his hair, he stood, keeping his back to her. "Let me deal with Drew."

His words made Blair shiver. "What aren't you telling me?"

"I'll deal with Drew."

Blair grabbed her T-shirt from the floor, and holding it in front of her, rose. The unyielding strength of Michael's back confirmed that he was holding back. "I deserve to know what's going on."

He bent to retrieve his boxer shorts off the floor. Only after putting them on did he face her.

"Drew's involved in the embezzlement."

Blair couldn't register what he was saying. "What?"

"I found evidence that ties Drew to the theft of a lot of money."

"You can't believe that. Why would Drew need more money? He has plenty from the estate."

"Do you believe I stole the money? Do you think I killed Hector Ramos?"

"Of course not!"

"You can't believe us both, Blair. One of us is a thief and a murderer."

"Both of you are innocent."

He shook his head, then pushed his hand through his hair again, "Hell, I don't know what to believe. But you can't talk to Drew until I talk to him."

Incredulous, Blair sat down. "You want to see if he would hurt me." She tried to take a breath, but felt her throat tighten. "He wouldn't hurt me any more than you would."

"Can you honestly say you've been safe with me? That I didn't endanger you? Got a little carried away when we got here?"

"You made love to me with desperation. I wanted that. You didn't hurt me."

"No, I almost got you killed."

"Damn it, Michael! I chose to help you."

"You should have been home, living your life, staying safe."

She'd been trying to hide from the fact that she loved him. "I was so scared the whole time. And now you're telling me that I can't trust my own brother?"

"Let me handle this my way, okay? Let me talk to him."

Michael was wrong. He had to be. "But if he won't listen to you, I'll talk to him."

* * *

Not if he'd hurt you to protect himself, Michael thought. But he agreed in order to placate Blair. He'd know soon enough if Drew could be trusted to protect her.

The hot passion of an hour ago had been replaced by a silent impasse. They showered and dressed in their same sweaty clothes. Room service brought them an early dinner and they left in search of a pay phone in the city.

Michael got Drew on his cell phone immediately. Only a few curt words were necessary to arrange a meeting. Michael asked for two hours, hoping Drew would believe he hadn't had time to check the beach, thereby giving Michael time to check the construction site he'd chosen for their meeting. He knew that also meant Drew had more time. But they had agreed Drew would come alone. That would be the first true test. If Drew was innocent and had any remaining faith in Michael, he would honor the promise he'd made.

Unless he really believed Michael capable of hurting Blair.

"What did he say?" Blair asked on the drive back to the hotel.

Michael chose not to give her Drew's exact words. They weren't fit for her ears. "That you'd better be all right, or he'd hurt me."

"If I go with you, he'll know I'm fine."

"I told him not to tell anyone, especially not James. But if he does, James will be there. I won't risk it."

"If Drew promised—"

"Blair, we don't trust each other. I have to work with that." With everything going against him, he prayed he didn't have to make any hard choices about Drew. He didn't want to hurt Drew, but if Drew couldn't, or wouldn't, take care of Blair, there would be no choice. Blair was Michael's only consideration.

They drove back to the hotel in silence. In their room, Blair sat by the window, curtains open, staring at the Atlantic, sipping a soft drink she'd bought from a vending machine. Michael knew he had to tell her what to expect, what to do, if things went wrong.

"Blair."

Blair jumped up, sloshing soda over her hand. She'd been day-dreaming, wondering what it would be like if things were normal. If she and Michael could just have time. Normal time. Not the insanity of the past days, not the magic of the single week six years ago. Time like other people. Those silly girlhood dreams.

"I didn't mean to startle you." He'd stopped pacing, something he'd done incessantly since they'd been back. She'd watched him surreptitiously at first. Loved watching him, until the wired grace of his strides told her just how worried he was. Now she feared where that worry had taken him.

"It's okay," she mumbled, using a tissue to wipe at the soda that had fallen to the carpet. She threw the tissue in the small trash can next to the desk.

"Why don't you sit down?" Michael offered.

Why did this feel like an executioner's request? Because he looked so grim? So serious?

So dangerous.

She managed to sit back down.

"If anything happens—"

"Michael—"

"If I don't come back, if you don't hear from me," his words were even, "by eight o'clock tonight, call Jimmy Sanchez."

Blair stared in dumbfounded silence as Michael handed her a slip of paper.

"This is his number. All you have to do is tell him there's a problem. He'll know what you mean."

Michael's bold handwriting stared at her. She wanted to take the scrap, ball it up, trash it.

"Trust him, Blair. Whatever he says to do, do it. No matter how insane, no matter how wrong you think he might be."

She looked up from the paper, feeling as if she were in a dark tunnel, Michael at one end, she at the other.

"Don't open the door for anyone. Not room service, not Drew, not anybody. Not even Jimmy unless you call him first."

She looked up at him, unable to form words.

"If you hear me, don't open the door unless I say—" He seemed to consider something for a second. "Estudiantes. Open only if I say Estudiantes."

She could do nothing but stare at him.

"Understand?" he demanded.

No she didn't understand. He was giving her a password?

He strode forward, taking the few steps necessary to stand directly in front of her. Kneeling, he held her upper arms and shook her lightly. "Understand?"

She nodded, caught in his dark-eyed gaze, pinned by his intensity.

"If it goes well with Drew, I'll bring him to you."

She nodded because he seemed to expect it, but inside she was numb.

* * *

Michael checked the Glock for what felt like the tenth time. Sore muscles and exhaustion were wearing him down. So was thinking too much.

Thinking about what might have been. About

mistakes, missed opportunities.

He stared at himself in the bathroom mirror. A man with more faults than he cared to enumerate stared back. Six years ago he'd wanted blind faith from Blair. He hadn't stopped to think about what, beyond money, she would be giving up to marry him, to come into his life.

What a damn joke. Except for his family, work was his life. He'd made it that way. What he couldn't remember now was if it had become his reason for living after Blair, or if he'd chosen to make it so before Blair.

She'd had every right to bolt then. If he lived through this and cleared his name, if Drew miraculously turned out to be innocent, his life would be as it had been. Not particularly safe, not the kind of life that brought him home to dinner every night. Not the kind of life that would provide Blair with what she was accustomed to.

And if he quit? What would he do? Live off of her?

It was impossible. She'd been right to refuse him.

Nothing had changed since then. Here he was again, wanting her faith. Of course she believed in Drew. Michael didn't. No matter that Drew had threatened him with an anatomically disgusting death if anything happened to Blair, though that did give him hope he could trust him with her.

Michael splashed cold water on his face. Leaning on the sink, he turned his head from side to side, stretching tense muscles. A catch in his shoulder made him rotate the joint.

"Let me rub your shoulder." Blair stood looking into the bathroom.

"It's okay."

"It won't take a second. Sit down." She walked in

and led him to the toilet, where he sat. He let her remove his dirty T-shirt.

Then he felt the soothing coolness of the lotion she'd found on the counter. With firm pressure, she rubbed his shoulders, then his neck. Her strong hands worked on the muscles of his back, rubbing away tension and remnants of pain from the shooting and the incident with the plywood at the beach. She avoided the now uncovered stitches of the knifing.

He leaned forward onto his thighs, loving the feel of her fingers, slick with lotion. He wished things were different. Wished he could turn around, pull her to himself and pour out his love for her.

But everything he was, everything that put him here, at this point in time, with pain and exhaustion pulling at him, made him the wrong man for her.

Wanting Blair Davenport wouldn't change that.

He was who he was. She deserved someone who could give her those things she needed. Not a man who wouldn't be there when she needed him, not a man who couldn't give her that perfect home and those beautiful children.

He grabbed her hands to still them. She stiffened at the contact.

"I have to go." He released her hands, afraid he'd hold on.

She stepped away, her eyes wary. "It's early yet."

"I need to scout out the area around the beach where I'm meeting Drew."

"Wouldn't it be better if you met here?"

"Trust me, Blair. I'm better off with people around. This place is about a mile away, close to a construction site. I'll have cover if I need it and enough people to keep both Drew and me honest."

"Drew wouldn't hurt me. He won't hurt you."

With no reply coming to mind that would satisfy her, Michael stood. "Lock the door and make sure the bolt's in place."

He pulled his shirt back on and walked out of the bathroom. He couldn't look at her. If he did he'd pull her in to his arms and never let go. "If I need to call you, I'll let it ring three times, then I'll hang up and ring again. Don't answer unless you hear the first three rings."

"Does anyone know we're here?"

"No. Not even Jimmy. But he knows what to do if he hears from you. Don't lose that paper."

He'd reached the door, knowing Blair stood only a few feet behind him. Temptingly close.

"Michael?"

The soft inflection of her voice got to him. Knowing he shouldn't turn around, knowing something inside would break, he did anyway.

God help him! She was the most beautiful thing he'd ever seen. Exhausted, she radiated courage and trust. What was he throwing away?

A life. He was throwing away their life because of a decision he'd made years ago. A decision that had led his own brother to his death.

Reaching out with one hand, he touched her cheek, traced the line of her brow, and pushed an errant strand of hair behind her ear.

Then the tearing inside was too much. He pulled her against him and held on for the times that hadn't been, all the times that wouldn't be.

Blair hugged him back as hard, and as desperately. He pulled away marginally, grasping her face with both hands, looking deep into her amazing eyes, and kissed her.

* * *

Blair heard the door click closed. It was over. He hadn't bothered with the words.

That's where he'd been going all along. She felt something give, something precious to her. That tiny hope she'd held so close, that this was their second chance. That she'd be braver, stronger. But this had nothing to do with her anymore. Michael was telling her they had no future. No matter what happened.

No future with him.

She'd been a fool six years ago. She should have done what her mother did: accept the man she loved despite the very obvious problems, the differences. She should have gambled and said yes to Michael's proposal. So life wouldn't be perfect. She could have had him for a time.

Now she had nothing.

* * *

Michael could still taste her. The sweetness of her, the giving. He could also taste the bitterness of finality. He thought he'd tasted that six years ago. But that parting was nothing to this one.

Blocking out the thoughts that ravaged his mind, he concentrated on driving. It didn't take long to get to the meeting place. He was about forty-five minutes early. He figured Drew was here, too. And possibly, James Meyer.

Michael parked the car in a lot on the beach side and made his way across the sidewalk where strollers and roller-bladers were enjoying the late afternoon breeze. Families with children played close to gently breaking waves. Off to the east, over the dark blue of the Atlantic, thunderclouds loomed huge.

He made his way around the bench where he and Drew had agreed to meet. Behind the bench, construction workers had already vacated a partially-built hotel, a perfect place for a sniper.

He made his way around to the side where the safety fence had been left open as an access point and went in. Not too much had been completed: two floors, with the third-floor wall supports in. He climbed to the second floor, knowing that would be the place he'd lay in wait if he were Drew.

He checked every possible hiding place, taking note of each with relation to the bench. It might help to know where the bullet with his name on it would come from. He stayed behind a pre-stressed support beam until he saw Drew park his car and make his way to the beach. He'd either decided it was pointless to scout the area, or had been too far away to get there early enough.

Unless he'd brought help. Eyes squinted against the sun low in the west, Michael looked for anything unusual. Long minutes later, after checking in every direction, he was as sure as he could be.

Drew had come alone.

* * *

Blair paced. She'd never in her life paced. This was what Michael had felt earlier, this itchiness, this need to move, to do something, anything, to get past the moment.

She tried to forget his last kiss. She'd wanted to beg him to walk away from the entire mess. They could have gone anywhere, hidden from the false accusations. The Davenport money would finally be put to good use.

But that would have proven her lack of trust. And ultimately destroyed Michael.

She moved toward the balcony and opened the sliding door. A brisk hot breeze buffeted her as she went to the railing in an effort to see if anything was being built to the north of the hotel, along the beach. But the hotel curved, so she could see nothing but more of the building, and on the beach, late afternoon sun worshipers.

A quick glance at her watch told her it was twenty minutes before the time Drew had agreed to meet Michael.

Determined to stay calm, she went to the bathroom and scrubbed her face.

The phone started ringing when she came out.

Counting, fingers poised over the receiver, her nerves jangling with each ring, Blair waited.

Too many rings.

* * *

With one last check of the Glock, Michael made his way back down to the beach. A group of people, a family from the looks of it, had thrown their blanket down about twenty-five yards from the bench. Drew, dressed in jeans, a dress shirt, and a wind breaker, looking less like an FBI agent than Michael had ever seen him during working hours, glanced around from behind sun glasses.

Not yet, he'd wait a few more minutes. Make sure Drew hadn't brought someone with him.

Ten minutes until the appointed time.

* * *

Blair stood paralyzed by the phone. Who had called? She'd finally decided to call the front desk with an elaborate reason as to why she'd missed the call, when she heard a knock on the door.

Mind scrambling with possibilities, she stared at the door. She'd been careful to throw the latch. If only she were close enough to look through the peep hole. But if she walked across the room, whoever was out there would know.

The maid?

Not this late, she thought.

She heard the knock again, a bit louder.

"Miss Davenport?" a male voice called. "I know you're in there."

Blair felt a hot flush, then cold fear.

"Open the door. I have Michael."

It had to be James Meyer. Or Eddie. Or his friend.

Desperate, she lifted the telephone receiver and dialed the number Michael had left her. The call went to Jimmy's voicemail.

"Miss Davenport. You don't have much time. I have Michael. Open the door," the man at the door said.

Frantic, she dialed Drew. The call went straight to his voicemail. She wanted to scream. Fumbling the phone book, she found the number for the FBI office. She punched out the numbers.

"There's nothing you can do but open the door," the man said again.

It took too long to be transferred to Drew's office. The dark menace of the man outside the door made the seconds crawl by. Without giving the female agent who answered the phone time to say more than her name, Blair blurted out what she hoped would help. "Tell Drew that Blair called. It's an emergency. There's a man at my door. He says he has Michael. I'm going to open the door." She gave the woman her location and told her where she guessed Drew might be before putting the phone down, without hanging up, hoping Drew's office would hear the man and what he had to say.

"Michael's a dead man if you don't open the door."

That was enough. Blair couldn't stand it anymore. She made her way across the room to the door and looked out through the peep hole.

James Meyer stood there.

"Where is he?"

"I have him in my car."

It was a trick. It had to be a trick.

But what if it wasn't? What if he had Michael?

"How do I know you're telling the truth?"

"There's one way to find out. Don't open the door and watch the news. Michael's body will be found in front of the hotel."

Terrified, with a prayer for deliverance, Blair opened the latch and turned the knob with shaky fingers.

James grabbed her immediately, twisting her arm behind her and pulling her into the hallway.

"I have a gun, Miss Davenport. No one can see it, but believe me, I'll use it on you and on anyone you try to talk to. So don't do anything to make me think you want to call attention to us."

He pushed her toward the elevator, his breath hot on her cheek.

Mercifully, no one was in the elevator. He held her arm in a vise-like grip until they reached the lobby, then he whispered, "Don't so much as look at anyone."

They made their way out to a black car parked at the curved entrance to the hotel. It looked so much like an unmarked car that Blair looked around for more law enforcement.

"Where's Michael?" Blair asked as James pushed her into the car on the driver's side.

"Move over."

Fighting the urge to scream, Blair asked again. "Where is he?"

Throwing his left arm over the steering wheel, James cranked the car. The gun, which Blair hadn't seen until now, loomed huge in his right hand. She scooted over as far as she could, eyes frozen on the gun.

He pulled away from the hotel and made a fast turn north, his gaze moving from Blair, to the rear view mirror, to the road ahead.

"Where is he?"
"That's what you're going to tell me."

Chapter Fourteen

Michael pushed the Glock into the back of his jeans. The feel of the cold metal made him wonder if he could really shoot Drew.

One last look around told him he was relatively safe. Drew had come alone.

Approaching from a group of people, Michael made his way toward the man who could save Blair.

Drew watched him, a predatory gleam in his eyes. "Where's my sister?" he demanded while Michael was still a good ten feet away.

"Safe."

"I never thought you'd hurt her."

"I wouldn't hurt Blair. Look at James Meyer, Drew. He's the threat." Michael came closer, his fingers itching to grab his weapon. "Unless you already know that and don't care."

"What the hell does that mean?"

"Did you set me up?"

A curse burst from Drew's mouth. "I set you up? What the hell kind of game are you playing?"

"If you didn't, James is the one playing games."

Drew's expression changed from angry to assessing. "What?"

"He shot at Blair."

"What?"

"He shot at Blair at the airport. I got her out of there."

"Why the hell would he shoot at Blair?"

"The only reason I can think of is that he's the one who set me up. Blair can give me an alibi for the murder of Hector Ramos. If James killed Blair, no alibi. He could get away with Hector's murder. If he's involved in that, then he set me up."

"If he was setting you up, why did he show me evidence that proved you'd set me up?"

"To throw us both off. To get away with embezzlement and murder. Hell, I don't know."

"You shouldn't have run."

"And leave myself wide open? No thanks." Michael took a quick look around, trying to see anything that might be out of place, something he might have missed earlier to indicate Drew had brought backup.

With deliberate care, Drew removed his sunglasses. "You're saying James did all of this."

"Yes."

"That he shot you."

"Yes."

"That he shot at Blair."

"Yes."

"But why kill Hector?"

"I'm guessing he got mixed up with Hector. Hector is probably the one who took the evidence I had. James wanted it, for whatever reason. He has to be the one, other than you, who's been chasing me. But Blair can prove I didn't kill Hector."

"I shouldn't have let her get away from me in Emerald Bay. I should have known she was helping you." Drew squinted against the setting sun. "What's between you two?"

Michael's stomach twisted in knots. He loved Blair Davenport with all his being, but all it had ever done for either of them was hurt. More sure of Drew, Michael continued. "You've got to get Blair out of here and keep her safe."

"What about you?"

"I want James Meyer."

The shrill sound of Drew's cell made Michael start.

Drew punched at the phone, tilting it up. "It's my office. I should check in just in case it's got something to do with you."

Michael looked beyond the people, trying to see any danger.

"It's no trick. I didn't bring anybody and didn't tell anybody I was meeting you."

"What about James?"

"Last I saw him, he was at the office, trying to figure out what had happened to you."

"Go ahead, call," Michael said. It was a huge gamble, but he had to start somewhere.

Drew dialed. "Cut me off. Reception's bad," he explained. "I'll try again in a few."

Still wary of each other, they walked toward Drew's car, Michael's hand on the Glock.

As if he knew Michael didn't trust him yet, Drew kept his hands well in view as they made their way between the people still enjoying the afternoon.

"Where's Blair?" Drew asked when they reached Drew's car in the parking lot.

"I'll take you to her. I don't want anybody in your office to know you have her. I have friends she can stay with if you don't have a safe place."

Drew reached for the door handle just as Michael caught a movement from the other side of the car.

"Hands on the roof," James Meyer's said, slightly crouched on the other side of the car.

Drew reacted first, stepping away from the car, his right hand going automatically to his shoulder holster.

"Don't, Drew," James said. "Blair will be really sorry."

Drew froze. "What the hell?"

"Do as you're told. Both of you, before I shoot her. Slide your weapons across to me, then put your hands on the roof."

Michael thought about options, tried to remember how good a shot James was. Would James be able to get off a shot before he pulled the Glock?

Then he saw James's trump card.

A .44 Magnum pointed at Blair's neck.

Drew already had his hands on the roof of his car by the time Michael slid the Glock across.

"Good. Let's find a place we can talk." The .44 steady on Blair, James looked around. Finally he shifted the revolver, effectively hiding it from public view, but still kept it aimed at Blair. "Over there," he said, "the construction site."

As James came around the car with Blair at his side, Michael looked over at Drew. He eyed the weapons which lay on the ground where James had pushed them, then cut his gaze back to Michael. Michael shook his head. Then he saw a minuscule movement. A movement that told Michael that while he now trusted Drew, he shouldn't have to begin with.

Drew was still armed.

"Start walking," James said to Michael and Drew. "I'm right behind you. Don't think you can do anything. You know I'll shoot her."

"I'm sorry, Michael," Blair said, her voice surprisingly strong considering the situation.

"It's okay, *niña*." Michael played back everything he knew about the construction site. There had to be a place where rushing James would work. Where the odds would be with them, instead of with a man who had no intention of letting any of them walk away.

"How touching, Michael. I bet Drew didn't know his baby sister had run off with you, did you, Drew?"

Out of the corner of his eye, Michael saw Drew's jaws clench.

"Why did you do it?" Drew asked.

"You should know motive is a simple thing. The money," James replied. "I need it. I caught on to Hector's little game when Michael asked me to check something out. Hector and I had an agreement. I arranged to take a cut in exchange for services."

"Which included killing Michael."

"Hector was supposed to take care of that, but chickened out. Michael had enough evidence to charge him. Hector would implicate me. I couldn't afford that."

"Only Hector got the flash drive and kept it. I came home while you were there hoping to find it," Michael interjected.

"Bad timing, Michael. I'd even checked to make sure you were supposed to be reporting in, so I wouldn't bump in to you. But, like you said, Hector had already gotten the flash drive. Which, by the way, I now have."

"What about the shooter at Emerald Bay?" Michael asked.

"Couple of guys Hector hired. They're history. Just like poor Hector."

They'd reached the opening in the gate to the construction site. Michael turned his gaze toward James, assessing his hold on Blair. "So you decided to implicate me when killing me didn't work."

"Well, you were supposed to die."

"Why implicate Drew?"

"I figured you would tell him you were clean and he'd believe you. He had to have a reason to believe you were up to your neck in it."

"So if I thought he'd tried to set me up, I wouldn't believe him," Drew filled in.

"It worked."

"If I'd thought Michael had done anything wrong, he would have been under arrest instead of free to run," Drew said.

Michael turned sharply toward Drew. So he hadn't thought the worst. Great time to figure out a friend was really a friend.

"Go to the right here," James ordered.

Michael stole a look at Blair. She walked stiffly, trying to stay as far away from James as he'd allow. James kept the revolver pressed to her side, his hold on her arm tight.

A pile of white construction sand blocked their way. On the other side, cinder blocks, stacked as high as their heads, backed to the fence. Rebar lay strewn between the cinder blocks and a stack of plastic-covered cement bags.

Drew tripped and fell, landing beside a short stack of cement bags, his left leg bent under him.

"Get up, Drew. Keep your hands out of the sand," James ordered.

Drew did. He rubbed his hip with his right hand, and used his left hand to pull a compact semi-auto pistol from the holster on his calf.

Now they were armed. But so was James, and he had the advantage. He had Blair.

Drew stood, still rubbing his hip, the pistol now in his palm, hidden from James.

Opportunity. They needed opportunity.

"Up ahead," James said. "Right around the corner here."

Michael's heart slammed into his ribs when he saw where James was taking them. A drainage pond. The perfect place to dispose of bodies.

"Now. Line up over there." James nodded toward the deep, water-filled pond.

"This won't work, James," Drew said.

"I think it will. Michael, in a desperate attempt to escape, shoots both you and your sister. Only he's mortally wounded and doesn't make it out. We're far enough away from the beach that no one will hear the shots. Your bodies will be found in the morning."

Shrill, insistent beeping pierced the site. James jumped and stared at the source. Drew's cell phone. "Turn it off."

Drew complied. "How did you find us?"

"I followed you out of the office. The rest was luck. I lost you and pulled in behind a car that looked like yours at the Fontainebleau," he told Drew. "I'd already figured Michael would go for a meeting at some point and that he'd choose a public place. The beach in front of the hotel seemed like a good choice, so I walked out and looked up just in time to spot Blair on the veranda. It took me a few minutes to figure out which room she was in, then it was easy to convince her to open the door by telling her I had Michael."

"I didn't tell him—"

"I just had to watch your face." He smiled. "She was so damn scared when I drove up this way. All I did was watch her reactions. When I pulled into the lot, there you were. "

Michael cursed himself for leaving Blair. If he'd had more faith in Drew, he wouldn't have left Blair at the mercy of James. Now she was going to pay for his mistake.

"You know, Drew," James said in a conversational manner, "if I were you, I'd be glad your sister won't have the chance to have anything more to do with

Michael. Can you picture him at home with the Davenports? Blair would be forced to give up everything. I bet he doesn't even know which fork to use. Your family would cut her off for associating with someone like him."

Michael let James's words roll off him. "I'm good for one thing, James. I can get you out of this mess. Out of the country. I have the connections."

James let the revolver slip marginally. "I can take care of myself."

"You won't be able to spend the money. You'll have to hide it. If I got you to South America, you'd be free. No hassles."

Drew's phone went off again.

"I told you to turn it off!"

"Sorry," Drew mumbled.

"Who's trying to call you?"

"The office."

"Did you tell them where you were going?"

"No, I—"

"I did," Blair said and felt James grab her hair and pull her head back.

"What?" he choked out.

"While you were pounding on the door," she wanted to look at James, but his hold on her prevented it so she focused on Drew. "I called Drew's office and told a woman agent where Michael and Drew were meeting."

Had she seen Drew shift something from his left to his right hand? A quick glance at Michael told her nothing.

Nothing except that he wasn't looking at her. He was watching James, with a small portion of his attention on Drew.

"Bitch!" James yelled into her ear and pulled at her hair again.

The next thing she knew, Blair heard a pop and felt herself pushed toward Drew. Stumbling, she went down on one knee and felt the crushing weight of something hit her. An instant of confusion surprised her, then she realized the weight was Michael, pushing her down on to the sand.

Several loud blasts filled the construction site. She felt Michael jerk, twice, then heard Drew yelling, but couldn't understand what he said.

Then mercifully, all was quiet.

Michael was too quiet, too still.

Blair tried to move, but couldn't. Michael's weight kept her pinned to the uneven sand. In the ringing silence, she heard crunching footsteps. Michael's arm, limp and heavy, blocked+ her view. Something wet and sticky pooled on her right shoulder and ran down her arm.

She heard someone groan, but it wasn't Michael. She would have felt anything he said.

She tried to muster her strength to get out from under his inert body.

Then she didn't have to. Michael was off, rolling to one side. She scrambled to her knees to see how he was. Blood covered most of his upper left arm. She ripped at his shirt and tried to find the source of the blood, but the material wouldn't give way. Struggling to breathe, she bent to him, her hands searching his neck for life. He had a pulse, but in feeling for it her hands found more blood. Turning his head slightly, she found blood on the back of his neck.

Shaking, she tore at the shirt she wore.

"That's enough, I think."

She stopped, her shirt-front clutched in her hands, and looked up. James Meyer. Oh, God!

"Drew!" she shouted, desperate to find him.

"He's down, too, Blair. Looks like your saviors failed."

Blair dared a look at Drew. He lay stretched out on his stomach, one arm dangling into the pit. She could see his back rising and falling with his uneven breathing.

And right next to a piece of lumber, half-hidden by a cinder block, she saw a gun. Drew's little gun. Had he shot at James? How many shots did he use? How many shots did a gun like that have?

God, she didn't know. She didn't know anything.

"Get up."

"I have to help them."

"There's little point, is there?" James held his gun steady on her. "I'm the only one walking away from this."

Blair felt her insides freeze. A numbing calm made her heart slow down. "Let me be with my brother, please." Her voice quivered.

James looked down at her, then at Drew. Blair held her breath.

"I guess it would look better if you were next to him when they find you. That way it would be obvious that Michael shot you both." He used the gun to wave her over.

Blair stood, her heart tripping again. The cinder block that obstructed James's view of the gun was on the other side of Drew, too close to the edge of the pit. Carefully, she stepped over her brother and sat down, her hand resting on the cinder block, as if for support.

"It won't hurt," James said as she settled down in front of the block. "I'll finish them off before I leave."

"That's kind of you."

James laughed. A high-pitched laugh. "Sarcasm!" He shook his head. "That's amazing." His right hand, the one with the gun, wavered for an instant.

Blair adjusted her legs and let her hand drop off the block to the sand.

What if it didn't fire? What if—

It didn't matter. He was going to kill her. If Michael and Drew were still alive, she was their only hope. He would kill her unless she took a chance.

"I'm sorry this happened. Really," James was saying. "Your brother and Michael are normally good at what they do. I guess their worry over you made them easy marks."

Blair felt the cool steel of the gun, rough sand sticking to her palm. Her finger sought the trigger.

"I'm sorry, Blair," James said.

Blair looked at him for half an instant. Long enough to look into his eyes. He did look sorry. He had trapped himself with his mistakes.

She pulled the gun up and fired. The recoil was worse than she'd expected. It jarred her. James looked startled. He held his gun steady. Terrified, the numbness of fear wearing off, Blair squeezed the trigger again.

Material flew from his left side. Funny, it looked almost like she'd seen in the movies. James staggered, his arm limp. Crazed gray eyes held hers. She didn't know whether to shoot him again or help him. He fell, heavily.

Sobbing, scrambling over the sand, avoiding Drew, she pulled the gun from James's grip. He stared at her for a moment, then closed his eyes.

* * *

Michael's arm burned. His head burned. No, it hurt. Ached.

Then it all came back. In a rush of panic, he sat up. To his left lay James Meyer, unmoving.

"Blair!" Her name came out sounding like a croak.

She wasn't here. Drew lay a few feet away, on his

stomach.

Blair.

Where was Blair?

Michael got to his knees, the world spinning. Somehow, he crawled over to Drew and checked his pulse. Not strong, but beating. Fighting waves of nausea and the ever-spinning world, Michael searched Drew for a wound. Blood ran dark and thick into the sand below Drew's stomach. Hot fire ran up Michael's arm as he rolled Drew over.

Blair. Her name screamed across his thoughts. Where was she?

Michael ripped at his shirt, jerking it off with his right arm since his left one was useless. He balled the cotton fabric, wet with his own blood, and pressed it to Drew's waist, where the bullet had gone in.

Crunching footsteps amid the chaos of the whirling world made him try to straighten.

Drew's semi-auto. Where the hell was it?

Turning his head, afraid he'd topple over, he searched the ground around James for his .44.

Nothing.

The steps came closer. More than one person. Running. Heavy breathing.

"Blair." He wasn't sure her name actually came out of his mouth.

She was running, tripping in her haste. Behind her ran a uniformed policeman, already shouting into the radio attached to his shoulder.

Gasping, she fell to her knees beside him. "You should," she stopped for breath, "lie down." Tears ran freely down her cheeks.

"I'm okay," Michael managed, his heart soaring now that she was here. Unhurt. "Press on Drew's stomach."

She pressed down on Drew when Michael released

his hold on the bloody shirt. Her gaze held his for an eternity, her chest rising and falling.

She was so brave. So strong. He tried to smile at her, tried to reassure her in that small way that her brother would be all right. But his face felt frozen. A black void hovered around the edges of his periphery.

"There's so much blood," she said in a shaky voice.

"Mine," Michael managed. "A lot of it's mine." The black threatened to engulf him.

She tore her gaze from her brother and looked toward him. Michael tried to hold her eyes, tried to focus on a tear that rolled down to her top lip. She swiped at it, leaving behind a smear of blood. Her brother's. His.

Not hers.

He let the black void take him.

* * *

Michael had been here before. It was quiet and warm. And so, so bright. Soothing.

A glittering calm settled over him.

He was more curious than before to investigate the tunnel ahead. Brighter lights called to him, pulling him forward. One step and he felt a loss. Another, and the loss became greater.

Ahead stood David, awash in brightness.

The light beckoned. Tempting him with a promise of peace.

Behind him he heard his name. A frantic sound, a desperate sound.

Drew was going back. Where were they?

Miguel Ángel.

The sound of his name made him turn. Pain stabbed at him, but he heard his name again and tried to ignore it.

Miguel Ángel.

A white form materialized. A soothing whisper of air, of sound. A looming presence that prevented him from looking back at David, at the tunnel. A guardian in white, determined to push him into pain.

* * *

"Got him!"

Blair heard the emergency technician's exhausted words and slumped to the rough sand.

She'd almost lost both Drew and Michael. Her cheeks felt sticky with dried tears.

The EMT shouted into his radio, something about time. How much time it would take to get to the hospital. The uniformed policeman took her elbow and tried to help her stand.

"Do you want to ride in the ambulance?"

"Yes, please." She grabbed at the man's arm, trying to steady herself.

"We've notified your brother's office. They'll take care of it from there."

Blair nodded. Her mother would get a phone call. Michael's parents would soon know. She stumbled behind Michael's stretcher, a tech straightening an IV line. Drew was already on his way to the hospital in an ambulance, lying inside some sort of rubber thing, an oxygen mask over his face. Another ambulance pulled up for James.

The siren drowned out her thoughts. Michael didn't move, his face pale. His oxygen mask had been hastily pulled on after a tech had stopped pumping air from a hand-held bag. Blair had seen all of this. On television. Not in life.

The ride proved too long. Twisted in the front seat, she could see each drop in the IV lines attached to Michael. He was too still.

Then they were there, pulling in next to the

ambulance with Drew in it. The doors swung open and helping hands pulled the stretchers out. Blair slid from the high cab in numb exhaustion and watched men and women in scrubs whisk Michael and Drew through sliding doors and down a corridor.

The policeman who'd helped her walked up. "Need a hand?" He smiled, but Blair could see his anxiety.

She reached out to him and let him support her until she got her legs working again. Inside, the blast of the air conditioner made her clothes clammy. The policeman nodded to a nurse, who scurried away and returned with a blanket. The policeman put it around Blair. It felt warm.

"Will you be okay?" he asked.

She nodded.

"Someone will be here to take your statement."

"Thank you. I'll wait here."

Minutes later Blair became aware of people staring at her. She pulled one arm from the warmth of the blanket and tried to straighten her hair. They looked away. A glance at her hands told her they were covered with drying blood.

More minutes, long, endless ones, and the double doors opened. A man in green scrubs, the doctor, Blair guessed, came out. "Davenport?"

"I'm his sister," she said, standing, pulling the blanket tighter.

"We've taken him to surgery. He's lost a good bit of blood. The bullet's in his abdomen. It'll probably take about two hours, maybe a little more. Unless there's a lot of damage, he should be okay."

Blair nodded. She'd call her mother.

"What about Agent Alvarez?"

"You know him?"

"Yes."

"Blood loss almost got him. He's in surgery, too."

Running footsteps resounded through the waiting room. A blond woman in her fifties ran toward them, her face ashen.

Michael's mother. She had to be. The cheek bones, the slant of her eyes, were feminine versions of Michael's.

"Alvarez?" she asked, her voice breaking.

"He's okay. Are you a relative?"

"His mother."

"He's in surgery to repair his arm. He probably has a concussion. Once he's stable, we'll move him to ICU. I'll let you know when you can see him." He turned toward Blair. "I'll let you know when your brother's out. You might want to go clean up. It'll be a while." He turned and headed for the doors. As he reached them he turned back. "Mrs. Alvarez?"

"Yes?" Michael's mother replied.

"Your son has a guardian angel."

Mrs. Alvarez nodded and sat down, her eyes frozen on the swinging doors.

"He said Michael would be okay. We just need to be patient," Blair said, sitting down next to her.

Mrs. Alvarez looked up at her. "You're Blair, aren't you?"

Blair nodded.

"I had a dream, when I was pregnant with Michael. Just once, I never dreamed it again. But I chose his name based on that dream." Her words were soft, soothing.

"His name is Miguel Ángel, isn't it?"

"Like Michael, the Archangel. It's pretty common in South America. His father doesn't like it. How did you know?" His mother asked. "He won't tell anyone."

"I heard it." On a whisper of wind.

Chapter Fifteen

Rhythmic beeping intruded on Michael's pain. Something pinched the skin below his nose. Dark swirled around and around. He drifted, aware of the beeping, aware of voices.

Memories flooded him, forced him to struggle to open heavy eyelids.

Blair.

He knew he'd said it, but his mouth wasn't working.

Okay, she's okay, he remembered.

Drew.

"Drew," this time he heard his own voice.

Something warm touched his hand, a woman's voice spoke. "He's okay, Mr. Alvarez."

* * *

Blair watched Carlos Alvarez, who'd arrived shortly after his wife. He was a striking man. Nearly as tall as Michael, with black eyes and dark hair, now graying. Now, hours later, he hugged his wife close as they listened to the doctor explain Michael's condition.

"The head wound is nothing more than a gash. He does have a concussion, but the biggest problem is his arm. The bullet broke the bone in his upper arm and severed an artery. That's why he lost consciousness so fast. It'll take a while, but he should be fine. From the looks of him he's had a rough time recently. He'll need physical therapy, but he shouldn't have any long-term complications if he does as he's supposed to."

"Can we see him?" Carlos Alvarez spoke beautiful, though accented, English.

"Yes, of course. Follow me."

Mrs. Alvarez pulled out of her husband's arms. "Can Blair come, too?"

"I thought Miss Davenport was related to the other agent," the doctor said.

"She is, but she and Michael are close."

The doctor and Mr. Alvarez both looked at her. Blair felt she should straighten her hair, brush off her clothes. She probably looked like she'd infect Michael with her filth. "I washed my hands," she said holding up her now clean hands.

The doctor half-smiled and nodded. "Of course."

Michael lay slightly propped up, wires and lines running from all sorts of machines to him.

A heart monitor beeped to one side, the display reassuring them that Michael was as well as could be expected.

Mr. and Mrs. Alvarez approached the bed, their hands clasped tightly together.

"*Dios mío, hijo*," Mr. Alvarez said, bending to kiss Michael's forehead. The tender move brought tears to Blair's eyes.

"He is so young, he has so much left to do." His mother touched his check, then brushed his hair back, before also kissing him. "I wish he would—"

"His life, Maggie. It's what we said. What we always told him. His life is his choice." Mr. Alvarez said squeezing her hand. "He is strong. He will be okay."

Michael's mother used her other hand to touch Michael's right one. "He squeezed my hand," she said around a sob.

Blair looked down to where Mrs. Alvarez's hand held her son's. She'd been too scared before to think. None of what happened was the sort of thing she could reason out. But now, standing here, safe, with Michael's heartbeat blipping a reassuring rhythm, it all came rushing at her.

She stepped to the other side of Michael's bed and touched the fingers of his left hand. She thought she saw his eyes flicker, but they didn't open. His arm was bandaged thickly, encompassing his entire shoulder.

He'd almost died. Any one of the many cases he would take during his career could kill him.

He was a born and bred risk-taker. Son of a woman willing to leave home and family to live in another country; of a man willing to do the same. Blair knew herself: her father was a Davenport, from old Virginia money, unwilling to give up his life style; her mother a woman willing to at least try to accommodate her life to please the man she loved. Now Blair knew she didn't even have her mother's courage because she couldn't stand by while Michael risked so much.

Her worry for him could compromise his safety, as it had at the construction site.

Looking at him, lying there, so still, wired to unimaginable machines, she suddenly knew she'd been fooling herself.

He'd been right to end it.

Her fear for him would be his undoing.

He would not die because of her.

* * *

Michael cursed the wheelchair they'd forced him to sit in. He'd tried pushing with his right hand, but the single-sided effort sent him sideways.

"Mr. Alvarez, we'll take care of the wheel chair," one of the nurses said. "Transport will be here shortly."

So he waited, wishing he could handle this alone. But it was too important to see Drew to wait until they'd let him go without help. If he had to wait, so be it.

Drew had a private room down the hall. Davenport money could move mountains. Michael was sharing his room with an older man who'd had carotid artery surgery. The man had been entertaining, if nothing else. He had served during the Korean War and told the most hilarious, ribald stories imaginable. He never told a real war story, but sometimes he would trail off and Michael could see the horrible memories buried behind his aging eyes.

While appreciating his roommate and enjoying the visits from his parents, brother and sisters, one person was very obviously missing. Though he'd met Beth Davenport, her daughter had not come to visit him.

After a surreal few days that had neither time nor space, days when he thought David was in the room telling him to quit being stupid, Michael woke to the realization that Blair was gone. She hadn't come to see him.

The hurt of her first rejection came rolling back in black waves that multiplied as the days wore on and she didn't come. Intellectually, he knew this emotion had a lot to do with his wounds and the drugs he was taking. He wasn't thinking clearly, so he asked to be taken off all pain medication.

Because as chivalrous and right as it was to know that Blair should have a life without him, Michael knew he was basically selfish.

He wanted her.

And he knew what it would take to get her and keep her. Well, he hoped he knew.

Drew was the first step.

Michael found him dozing. The orderly who'd finally pushed him down the hall left them and Michael sat quietly for a few minutes.

Drew woke up with a start and stared at him. "You okay?" he asked.

"Yeah. How about you?" Michael replied, shifting his left shoulder to ease the ache in his arm.

Drew smiled. "Well, they tell me I won't need a colostomy bag, so I'm feeling pretty damn good."

Michael smiled back.

Drew pushed a button and raised himself to a sitting position. "I've thought about what happened. I should have told you what I was doing to figure out how our names got into the bank records."

"It looked pretty bad, Drew. I'm not sure I would have believed me."

"Yeah, you would have." He paused. "The only names that kept popping up were yours and mine. I knew you wouldn't be so stupid as to leave information about yourself on records you'd tampered with, but there was nothing else to go on."

"James was pretty good. How's he doing?"

"He'll be okay. He's lucky Blair's not a better shot."

Michael nodded. He didn't give a damn if James Meyer lived or died, he just didn't want Blair to be the one to have ended his life.

"You read me pretty well back there. I only took the shot at James when I saw you were going for Blair." Drew shook his head. "Then I missed the son of a bitch."

"That was a tough shot."

"I should have got him. Would have saved us both a lot of pain and Blair a lot of agony."

"How is she?"

Drew's eyes narrowed. "She hasn't been to see you?"

"No."

Drew looked surprised. "What did you say to her?"

"Say to her?"

"The last time Blair talked to me, she all but admitted she was in love with you. So what the hell did you say to my sister?"

Michael supposed he was glad Drew couldn't get up. But it might have felt good to have someone pound some sense into him. "I thought she could do better than me."

"That's the stupidest thing I've ever heard. What the hell were you thinking?" Drew didn't wait for a reply. "Do you love her?"

"More than anything." That was why he was here.

"My sister isn't going to come running back to you."

"She's smart. I don't expect her to."

"She'll try to get over you by challenging herself to something." Drew seemed to assess him for a moment. "I suspect that's how she did it before. There was a before, wasn't there?"

From the fierceness in Drew's eyes, Michael was glad his friend was on his back.

"Yes," he said, shifting in the wheelchair, uncomfortable under Drew's scrutiny. "I screwed up back then. But I won't again."

Five minutes later, after getting to the real point of his visit with Drew, Michael turned the chair around. "I'll talk to you later."

He managed to get the wheelchair through the door awkwardly until an orderly spotted him. He could have stood up and walked, but he'd been given an opportunity he wasn't going to lose.

He'd accept the wheelchair. For now. He wasn't going to risk a chance with Blair because of stubbornness or pride. He'd taken care of some things that might stand in their way.

He wanted a future.

* * *

222

Blair pushed the vacuum cleaner across the carpet. Drew's apartment had become her focus of attention. She'd spent the first few days after the shooting at the hospital and here, helping her mother deal with a jumble of half-paid bills Drew had ignored for too long. Drew had seen his invalid status as the perfect opportunity to deal with bills and paperwork, but Blair and Beth knew he wasn't thinking clearly yet, so they'd straightened out the problems.

Now Blair found herself cleaning. Physical activity always made her feel better, though dealing with Drew's bedroom wasn't something she wanted to repeat. Just to be able to walk, unimpeded, she'd spent a few hours clearing the floor of dirty clothes and old shoes. It amazed Blair that Drew could live like this when they'd grown up with such order.

Of course, the order hadn't been of their making but the responsibility of several servants.

Still, he couldn't have been happy like this. She shoved the vacuum down the hall. It stopped suddenly. She stood it upright and stared, then realized she'd probably stretched the cord too far. She looked back toward the wall socket.

The doorbell rang.

Hopefully it wasn't another of Drew's neighbors. It seemed like every woman in the apartment complex had decided she would make something sweet for Drew to eat when he got home. If he ate everything, he'd collapse from sugar overload.

She left the vacuum and went to the door, looking through the peek hole.

Michael.

Stunned, she stepped back.

She would ignore him. Silently, she backed further away.

"I know you're in there, Blair," he said quietly.

Why couldn't you stay away? Why couldn't you leave me alone?

"Blair, open the door." He paused. "Please."

"What are you doing here? You should be in the hospital."

"Well, I'm not. So how about letting me in before I fall over?"

Did she detect laughter in his voice? That really made her angry. She jerked the door open. "What are you doing out?"

He looked awful. Thinner, tired. His left arm, still thickly bandaged, lay in a sling.

Only his eyes danced with light, his mouth turned up in a half smile. "I thought you were going to leave me out here at the mercy of Drew's neighbors."

She held on to the door for support. "You should be in bed."

"You wouldn't come see me." The words held no accusation, but she felt guilty just the same.

He met her gaze, holding it too long, as if in challenge, then carefully made his way through the narrow opening she'd left between the door and the frame. Blair stepped back and watched him ease onto Drew's couch, the whole scene so reminiscent of his arrival at Grandma Alice's that she wanted to cry.

She'd been a fool to let him in. She felt ragged, exhausted from the effort of trying to keep herself from rushing to the hospital to see him.

She stood by the open door.

"I'm not going away, Blair."

That made her close the door and face him. "You should have stayed away."

"We've never really talked about us."

"There's never been an us." She was sure her voice

shook.

"No, I ruined it six years ago."

"There was nothing to ruin. It was a week. A flash in the pan." God, how saying those words hurt.

"I shouldn't have asked you to marry me—"

"I really don't want to hear this—"

"Listen to me, Blair."

She turned away.

"Please."

She didn't want to do this. It was enough that she'd fooled herself into thinking there might be a chance for them. But to have him come and tell her he shouldn't have proposed was too much.

Reluctantly, she turned toward him again.

"I shouldn't have asked you to marry me then because it was wrong not to consider your feelings." He drew in a breath. "Remember how I told you we all pretend?"

Somehow, she nodded.

"I wanted it all, Blair. I wanted you and the job of avenging David. I needed to hold on to something stable so I wouldn't have to accept that David was gone. But I didn't want to admit to those feelings. I was pretending to cope, so I could do what I had to do. Meeting you gave me something I thought I could control, something I could make work. Not like David's death. I asked you to marry me for all the wrong reasons. If you had accepted, you would have paid the price for my selfishness."

Blair didn't know what to say. Her thoughts crowded in on themselves.

"I'd never been in love before," Michael continued. "I'd always sort of played at it, you know? And there you were. This beautiful girl I couldn't keep my hands off. I thought if I showed you excitement, you'd fall in love with me, too."

She sat down across from him, in Drew's recliner. "You never said—"

"I never said I love you." His eyes burned into her. "No, I didn't. I guess I wanted you to say it first. I thought you'd say it after I asked you to marry me. Your answer floored me."

She'd struggled for so long to forget that day, but Michael's words brought it all back.

"We'd just made love. In the car, Blair," his voice dropped. "It was incredible. We'd risked being seen, we both knew people ran along Sunrise Cove, but we couldn't stop."

Oh, God, how she remembered.

His deep voice continued. "It hurt, it was so unexpected, when you said no."

She wanted to tell him she was sorry. Explain how many times she'd regretted the decision. Explain how many other times she'd known it was the right thing to do.

"I regretted asking you. I regretted everything I said. When you didn't call, I imagined that you were pregnant and alone. I started to call, then Drew mentioned that you were back in college and he didn't seem upset, so I reasoned you weren't pregnant. I spoke with Alice and she never said a word, though I think she knew something happened between us."

"I should have called. You would have known then."

"I left you in anger, Blair. I didn't expect you to call." He leaned forward, adjusting the sling across his chest. "I never expected to fall in love. I don't think I admitted it was love until I saw you again. Admitting it would have made me accept David's death and make hard choices about life."

Michael took a deep breath. He could tell he'd

wounded her with his honesty. But she had to understand. "You're a Davenport. I'm the guy looking for excitement, looking to prove myself. I worked for that from the time I left high school. Then I joined the Bureau, David died and, bang! There you were. Beautiful, rich Blair Davenport. Who didn't need me for anything."

She looked back at him with her eyes wide, her mouth trembling.

"I needed you," he said softly. "I needed you to provide an anchor for me after David."

A single tear rolled down her cheek. She said, "You scared me to death."

"How?"

"All that energy. You lived every moment so completely. I couldn't hope to keep up."

"It was all I had to give. After you, those things we did, flying, sailing, sitting on a damn porch, none of those were the same. The excitement wasn't in doing them. It was in being with you, but I'd been too stupid to know it."

"But those things are a part of you. It was your dedication to your job I couldn't hope to compete with or live with."

God, what a fool he'd been. "I should have explained things."

"I can't tell you it would have made any difference." She took a ragged breath. "I clung to this dream of what my life would be, sort of waited for it to come and get me."

"There's nothing wrong with that."

"After you, I realized I had to take control of my life."

"But you had everything."

"Except purpose." She looked down at the floor for

a few moments. "If I'd said yes to you, I would have fallen in to this pattern of dependency. You would be my world." Her gaze sought his. "And you weren't going to be there. You were going away."

"I made a mistake, Blair. A horrible one that kept us apart. We could have worked it out."

"No, Michael. We couldn't have. Because as much as I wanted to say yes to you, I knew I couldn't make me work in the relationship. There was no me."

He was too scared to ask. But she was worth the risk. "What about now?"

Her breath caught. "You love what you do. My fear would be nothing but a millstone around your neck."

He'd had a lot of time to think during the days when she'd stayed away. He'd been right. He'd understood her reasons. "There are other jobs."

She shook her head, her eyes so sad. "They're not for you. This is for you. Remember, I saw you, hurt, on the run, trying to figure out what was going on. You have to have that challenge."

"There are other challenges, *niña*. I talked to lots of people, had friends pull strings. I've put in a request for a change of duty that's been granted. I'll be on a bank robbery task force, no more undercover."

"Is that what you want?"

"Yes." He was sure of it. "The job will be a new challenge." He tried to smile, but wondered if his lips had turned up in desperation or humor. She could still say no.

"Then you'll love it."

Now. He had to do it now. While he still had the nerve. "I love you, Blair. I don't want you sitting home waiting for me. I want to grow old with you. I'm not going to do anything to risk that. This job's as safe as it gets." He paused, sure he had her full attention, scared beyond belief. "Will you marry me? Will you start a brand new life with me? One we can build together?"

Blair wondered if her mouth were hanging open. Never, even in her wildest dreams, had she imagined—dared hope—that Michael would ever want anything other than the thrill, the danger.

"After the past month" he continued, "I don't think I have it in me to expose myself to getting hurt again. The arm's going to heal, but I'm thirty-five. It's time to concentrate on a future."

"But you love the work. You love the chase."

"That part won't change, but I don't want to deliberately put myself in the line of fire anymore. I don't know how long I haven't wanted it. Maybe for the past six years. I did it because it was what David and I wanted growing up. Part of the rush. It was what I expected. I never expected to meet you."

Blair focused her attention on his eyes, so intensely dark.

"I want you, Blair. A real life with you."

A tiny sliver of hope shone in the dark that had been her life for days. "I don't want to be responsible for making you change your life."

"There's no getting away from that. You have. Loving you has changed it. I want to change my life. I want you. But even if you refuse me again, I won't go back to the risks I took."

She looked at him, sitting so still on her brother's couch, his left arm immobilized. She'd loved him from the moment she'd seen him, from their first dance at Mitzi's party. She'd loved him when she refused his proposal, loved him when he showed up at the beach, loved him when he lay unconscious in the hospital. She would love him even when there was no breath in her body.

"Then you'll need someone to come home to at night." She hoped the little quiver in her voice hadn't been as pronounced as it sounded. He'd given up the most dangerous aspect of his job. No, he wouldn't be one-hundred-percent safe, but she could live with this.

Michael smiled. That heart-warming smile she wanted all to herself. "Does that mean—?"

"I love you, Michael." She took a deep breath. "Yes, I'll marry you."

He turned serious, his eyes on her face. "Then you'd better come here, *niña*. I think I used up all my energy on the way over."

Blair stood on shaky legs and slowly made her away toward the couch. It was the final journey. She sat down next to him and he shifted to put his right arm around her.

"I'm hurt worse than I was after the knifing." He sounded so serious.

"I know."

"What my body says it can do and what it can really do, might be at odds for a few more days."

She smiled. "I'll take my chances."

Epilogue

"Do you want to go out for dinner, Mrs. Alvarez?" Michael's voice intruded on Blair's dream.

"Hmm?" Memory and desire mingled warm and heavy in her consciousness.

"Do we go out for dinner?" he asked again.

Behind closed lids, Blair pictured the small church where they'd been married. Michael's cousin, a priest, had flown in from his hometown in Argentina to officiate. Both of their families had been present, even the stodgy Davenports, her father's family. Grandma Alice and Blair's mother had cried. Blair wondered what it had cost Uncle Benjamin, her father's uncle, to attend a wedding and reception swarming with what he called 'common' people. But he'd done it. Probably to keep up appearances. To everyone's immense relief, Michael's father and Uncle Benjamin had somehow hit it off. Michael's brother and sisters had been a riot to meet, all energetic and fun.

They were on the second day of their honeymoon. In a few days, they'd head back to Miami.

"Blair?"

But Blair ignored the softly spoken word. Bits and pieces of the last month and a half fell in to place. Destiny and life combined into reality.

Through the west window, the sun setting, a golden ball falling into the Gulf. Grandma Alice had insisted they use her house for their too-short honeymoon.

"I'm starving," she said, smiling. Then she felt it. A little unsettled, very unexpected. "But I don't feel so good." Again. She bolted for the bathroom.

Minutes later, after splashing cold water on her face and brushing her teeth, she came out, feeling much, much better. Michael stood waiting, naked and impatient, the sling supporting his left arm back in place. "Are you okay?"

"Oh, yes."

"That didn't sound okay."

"It's better than okay."

"Blair?"

She reached up and touched his face, tracing the line of his brow.

"Remember how we wondered why I hadn't gotten pregnant before?"

He stared down at her. "Good God."

"It was timing. And destiny. This is our time, Michael."

"You're pregnant," he said, wonder in his voice.

"If I had to guess when, I'd say the Fontainebleau."

He reached down and touched her bare stomach, still flat. "Destiny and timing," he repeated. Then he traced his hand back up her body to her face. "And more love than I ever imagined." He kissed her gently.

When he pulled away, his eyes reflected mischief and humor. "I can't remember what happened at the Fontainebleau." He pulled her against him, his body, if not his memory, obviously functioning properly. "Does this pregnant woman feel up to...?"

Author's Note

Thank you for reading *Against the Wind*. I hope you enjoyed it! I'd love to hear from you. Please drop me a note at virginia@virginiakelly.net

* Would you like to know when my next book is available? You can sign up for my newsletter at http://www.virginiakelly.net/news.html or follow me at http://amazon.com/author/virginiakelly
* Reviews help other readers find books. I hope you'll take a moment to leave a review
* This is the first book in a stand-alone series. The next two are *Just One Look* and *Take a Chance on Me*

Best wishes and happy reading,
Virginia

SPECIAL NOTE: PS: Hurricanes are neither fun nor romantic. They are dangerous. If you live in or visit an area that experiences hurricanes, be aware of the forecast during hurricane season, which runs from June 1 through November 30. Know if you are in an evacuation area and be prepared to leave if directed to do so. If you are not in an evacuation area, you should be able to manage for three days without outside help. This includes water, food and medicine. The National Hurricane Center has further information, both in English and Spanish.

About the Author

Virginia Kelly's first story involved a mouse that hitched a ride with Paul Revere. She was eleven. A bit later, dreams of romance (with requisite happily ever after), adventure, and danger came together to produce her RWA Golden Heart nominated novel. Her books have been nominated for several awards including the Holt Medallion, the Golden Quill, the Aspen Gold and the National Reader's Choice Awards. She writes about dangerous heroes (sexy, gorgeous ones, of course!) and the adventurous women willing to take a chance on them. An academic librarian, Virginia is a native of Peru and lives in Florida with her family. To learn more about her books and check out her travel photos, visit her website at http://virginiakelly.net

See the next page to begin reading chapter one of the next book in series.

Just One Look
Chapter One

Saint's Island
North Florida Gulf Coast

FBI Special Agent Drew Davenport wanted to punch something. Pitch boulders off a mountaintop. Have hot, sweaty sex with Scarlett Johansson. On the floor.

Yeah. He was antsy and bored to death.

No, he quickly corrected, not to death. Death had been a near thing six weeks ago. He still wasn't completely back from that little fiasco, even if he refused to admit it to anyone. Which was why he was stir-crazy. He couldn't do what he normally did.

Work. Run. Hell, move with some degree of normalcy. At least normal enough to get him off desk duty.

He felt trapped in the tux jacket he'd struggled into for his sister's wedding. Since he'd had the staples out of his stomach, he had more freedom of movement, but damn, why waste that freedom wearing a tux?

But he had to give Blair credit for choosing to be married on the island just off Emerald Bay. They'd spent so much time at their grandmother's Gulf Coast beach house that the area was like a second home. He and the wedding guests, almost exclusively family, were lodged at a very nice resort hotel on the island. He could look forward to days of sun, sand, and blue water. All of which would probably be good for him, recuperative.

Lots of people? Not so much. At least Blair's husband-to-be, Michael Alvarez, was a friend, despite what had gone down just a few weeks ago. But his whole family? Hell, Drew just wasn't up to dealing with all those strangers. Other than his sister, mother and grandmothers, his own family—God help them all, Uncle Benjamin at a wedding—was too much.

Michael's family, some of whom he'd met while he was in the hospital, others last night at the rehearsal dinner, seemed nice, friendly. The younger sister, over the top bubbly, had exhausted him. The older one should have been seated next to Uncle Benjamin. Well, his sister was marrying into the family, not him. Their brother, military, hadn't arrived, but was due today.

A knock on the door interrupted his thoughts.

"Drew?" his mother called. "Are you dressed?"

"Coming, Mom," he replied, resigned to the beginning of the insanity of wedding day.

She beamed at him when he opened the door. She was thrilled that Blair was marrying the man she loved. And she looked, well, gorgeous.

His mother was gorgeous. Wow. Why hadn't he noticed before?

She came in and hugged him, holding on a bit longer than he'd expected.

"I love you, Drew," she said, and he heard tears in her voice. "How are you feeling?"

"I love you, too, Mom," he replied. She'd been beyond worried when he'd been shot. Blair told him she'd stayed by his bedside round the clock. Sometimes he thought he remembered seeing her. "I'm okay, really." He'd probably repeated that phrase twenty times a day since he'd gotten out of the hospital.

She stepped back, but took his hand. Yep, tears in her eyes. One escaped her attempts to blink it away and rolled down her cheek before she could stop it.

"Aw, Mom. Don't cry." As usual, he was helpless in the face of tears.

"I'm not," she protested. "I just—"

"What?"

"I want you to take the time, Drew. Please. Get well, use it to..."

"To?"

"Recover."

"I'm recovering," he insisted.

"I saw you running this morning. Are you sure you should?"

"Mom, I'm not one hundred percent. I know that, but I have to get back in shape to do something other than sit at a desk." And work wasn't his only concern, because if Vicky Holland, the downstairs neighbor with good intentions, an amazing imagination, and the hottest body ever couldn't get a rise out of him, he had another problem. But no way in hell was he talking about that with his mother.

"Recover slowly. Don't rush going back to work. Have other priorities."

"Work is my priority."

"Michael has found there's more to life than the FBI, Drew. Maybe you should follow his example."

He shook his head. "Mom."

"Okay, okay," she said, still sounding too close to

tears for comfort. "Do you need help with your tie?"

"I think I can manage. Do I have to wear the cummerbund?"

"Andrew Sloan Davenport," she said before adding the clincher, "the Third. There isn't a cummerbund. Didn't you check the tux?" Now she sounded like a pesky mother.

"Great." Of course he hadn't checked the damn tux. He'd gotten out of having it fitted because he and Michael were close enough in size that he'd told the rental place to use whatever size he chose.

"Blair's dressed and left. You should, too."

"It won't take me as long as it did her."

"Michael's dressed."

"Michael's the groom. He's anxious to marry my little sister."

"Everyone else is dressed and ready."

"Is Uncle Benjamin ready?" he countered.

She laughed. They both knew his great uncle functioned under his own rules. "Yes, he's talking to Michael's father in the family suite."

"Really." Interesting. Uncle Benjamin spoke only to those he considered of his "class." Rich. Michael's father wasn't. The fact that Carlos Alvarez was an engineer didn't figure into Uncle Benjamin's calculations. Only old money counted.

A knock, followed by a male voice asking, "Drew, you in there?" had his mother opening the door.

Michael Alvarez greeted her with a hug and stepped inside. His dark hair was combed, his tux perfect, but he looked harried. He still wore the sling on his left arm, a legacy of the shootout. He turned to Drew. "We need to leave." He glanced at his watch. "Now."

"A little tense, brother-in-law?"

"Don't tease him, Drew," his mother admonished.

"Ceremonies are stressful enough."

She would know. Davenports were big on ceremony.

"I'm going to the car," Michael said. "If you take longer than five minutes, I'll get a ride with someone else." With that he said a quick goodbye, pivoted and left.

"He's cranky, isn't he?" Drew said.

"He's nervous, honey. I'm sure it's been a challenge meeting the Davenports, even if Blair was there to mitigate the worst of it."

Just as much a challenge as when she'd met the Davenports herself, Drew figured.

"Please," his mother said, "get to the church before Uncle Benjamin. I'm afraid of what he'll say to Michael's family."

"Michael's family will be fine."

"I don't want anything to mar this wedding. I adore the Alvarez family. They're so down to earth."

Not rich snobs. That's what she meant. The Davenports were snobs. His mother had had a hard time fitting in her entire married life. Even after his father died, she still struggled even though the obligations of her position in the family were fewer.

"I'm nearly ready." Yeah, all he had to do was fix his tie. Why didn't the tux come with a clip-on? He didn't need another challenge.

Hell, the bow tie was only the smallest of his challenges.

"Doesn't Blair need you?" he asked.

"I'm driving over with your grandmothers in a few minutes." She looked at him, concern in her eyes. "Are you sure you don't need help with the tie?"

It was on his lips to tell her he didn't need anyone's help, but that would hurt her feelings. She'd been hurt enough when he'd been shot.

"Please," he said. Her answering smile made her face light up which made him feel like he'd done something right for a change.

For things to be right for him he had to get to work again. Once the wedding and reception were over, he'd be on track to getting his life back. That was all he needed.

No distractions. No more people he loved caught in the crossfire.

In other words, no more screw-ups.

* * *

Mia Alvarez pulled her hair back to begin the French braid she and her sister Izzy had decided would work best for them as bridesmaids.

"Mia," Izzy said with a huff. "I can't do this!"

"Let me do mine and then I'll do yours," she replied. She was good at this. One of her few remotely artistic endeavors. Over, under, repeat. Done.

If only straightening out the mess her life had become was as easy as braiding hair. But Michael's life, that was good. Their brother was alive, thank God, recovering from a shooting that almost killed him. After a nightmare of false accusations and a race for his life, he was marrying the love of his love on a beautiful Gulf Coast barrier island.

"Have you gotten a good look at Blair's brother?" Izzy asked.

"Mm, hmm," Mia replied pulling back Izzy's hair.

"Nice, huh?"

"If you like the stuck up type."

"He didn't seem stuck up to me," Izzy said.

"That's because you were worshiping him like he was some sort of god." Typical of Izzy and any guy that looked half-way decent.

"I was not!"

6

Izzy's was not response was also typical—a refrain they'd all heard growing up. Mia wished her younger sister would act her age. Twenty-two was way too old to continue with the nonsense of was not.

But she wouldn't tell Izzy that. Izzy would cry. Their mother would be upset, their father would try to mediate an argument that wasn't an argument, and there would be another family crisis. Her sister seemed to thrive on family crisis. When there wasn't one, which there mostly weren't, Izzy created one.

Crisis was David getting killed. Crisis was Michael on the edge of death. Crisis was not a silly argument.

Her job loss certainly wasn't, but she hated to think what Izzy would do if she found out what precipitated it. And how that would play out in the family.

"All that blond hair," Izzy sighed, ignoring her.

"His hair is brown," Mia replied. "A light brown."

"Honey blond," Izzy argued.

Mia refused to reply. Instead, she repeated over, under as she finished Izzy's braid.

"Ouch!"

"Sorry," Mia said. Maybe she'd pulled a little too hard, but Izzy's hair was so smooth it had slipped. "Almost done." She fastened and tucked. "There."

"Thanks," Izzy said, turning this way and that to admire herself in the full length mirror in the hotel room they were sharing.

She bore admiring. Pretty, with a perfect figure, she attracted men like the proverbial moth to flame.

"And it is honey blond. And he has beautiful green eyes."

"He's perfect then," Mia agreed with a smile. No point in arguing when Izzy was like this.

"I bet he'll be gorgeous in a tux. I'm so glad Michael relented and let this be formal."

Michael gave in to pressure from the snooty Davenports, not from Blair. Well, Mia admitted, Blair and her mother weren't snooty. But the rest of them? Yep. Snooty with a capital S. Maybe the grandmothers weren't so bad either. But the brother? Stuck up only mildly described him. Except for toasting the bride and groom, he'd kept to himself and barely said two words the whole evening.

And the uncle. Good God, the uncle. He didn't bear thinking about.

At least the setting was beautiful. She'd missed the rehearsal, but according to her mother and Izzy, the church was gorgeous, with a view of the Gulf of Mexico. The hotel, a resort, where families and friends were lodged, was right on the beach, with its sugar-white sand, and had given them a discount, otherwise Mia would have had to explain her situation to her family long before she intended to.

"Did you see Blair's gown? She says her mother helped her pick it out, but it's not frumpy or old looking at all."

"Why would Blair's mother choose an old looking, frumpy dress?"

"Because she's rich and rich people have oodles of money but are so stuck on proper attire—" Izzy said the last two words in a stilted British accent, "—that they pick stuffy clothes. Stuffy, like them."

"Well, neither Blair nor her mother are like that, which is good for Michael."

"He loves her, doesn't he?"

"Yes, and it shows," Mia replied. Blair and Michael were lucky, and Izzy? Well Izzy had no idea how many absolute jerks were out there.

"That's what I want," Izzy said in a dreamy voice. "A guy who loves me as much as Michael loves Blair."

Dream on, Mia thought. Other than her brothers, whose overprotectiveness drove her crazy at times, experience had taught her that most guys couldn't be counted on to do more than leave misery in their wake.

Her ex-boss was only the latest example.

She closed her eyes briefly and tried to forget the crazy notion that she'd seen him in the lobby earlier.

That was silly. No way would he follow her here. He wouldn't dare, not after she threatened to call the police if he didn't leave her alone.

She was just being paranoid.

* * *

Drew's mother had been so happy, so glad to be able to help him with his tie, that he'd thanked her with a hug that brought more tears to her eyes. And he meant the hug for all the times he hadn't called, hadn't even thought about her while he was working. He wouldn't forget to call, not again. He'd seen the fear in her eyes when he'd woken up in the hospital.

Hell, he was getting morose. Recovery was shitty. The doctor had actually said that to him.

Michael, two of his cousins and an uncle, had ridden with him to the church. Now, as he got out of the rental he'd picked up at the airport when he'd arrived, he straightened carefully.

Yeah, Michael was a good guy. Drew still felt like crap about believing, for even one second, that Michael had done anything wrong. Never mind the disaster that almost cost them their lives. From which Blair managed to save them.

While he'd been useless. As useless as he was now.

Michael's father met them in front of the church, after driving Michael's mother and two sisters. "Are you ready, hijo?"

Michael, fidgeting in his tux, asked, "Do you have

the rings?"

"*Caramba, hijo.* I'm not so old I forget things," Carlos Alvarez said. "Tell him to quit worrying, Drew. The boy is driving me crazy." But he laughed and hugged his son when he said it and Drew saw first-hand different the Alvarez family was from his. While he'd never questioned his father's love, Andrew Davenport would never have joked like this with him. It wasn't done. Even after Drew's mother had softened some of the aristocratic edges off, his father had still been reserved.

"Michael has reason to worry, Carlos. He's marrying my hard-headed sister."

"Blair will need to be hard-headed to deal with my stubborn son," Carlos replied.

The cousins, two brothers who'd flown up from Argentina with several other family members, added more comments to Michael's faults and the group laughed.

The younger sister stood in front of the church with four other women and the flower girl. Slim and pretty and so immature she made Drew's teeth ache, she'd been a handful last night at the rehearsal dinner. Only good manners had kept him in his seat. He was going to stay far, far away from the drama queen today. He tugged at his shirt collar careful not to mess with his tie.

That's when he saw her.

The knock-out, fiddling with the younger sister's hair. Who could that be? He'd met everyone, hadn't he? Both sisters, the endless cousins and assorted relatives. Who the hell was she?

She turned, and Drew knew instantly who she was.

The older sister. The prickly one with thick glasses. Mia, she'd said as she'd shaken his hand with ice-cold fingers and a businessman's grip. Only she wasn't wearing the thick glasses she'd worn at the rehearsal dinner, nor the prim business suit. She stood next to the younger sister... Izzy, that was it. Dizzy Izzy, he'd thought last night. She stood next to Izzy as calm and serene as a queen in a knee-length cream-colored dress that enhanced everything the business suit had hidden.

She wasn't tall or blond, what he'd always considered his type. Prepared to dismiss her since he'd been fooled too many times by good looks, he nearly turned away. Then she smiled at something the flower girl, daughter of one of the cousins, said, and squatted to be eye level with the little girl.

And all the prim, all the regal, disappeared.

She was simply breathtaking.

He remembered watching one of the old Godfather movies and ridiculing how, based on a single look, the youngest Corleone son had gone bat-shit crazy over a girl.

His rational self argued that this sort of thing didn't happen.

Still, he watched as she totally disregarded formality, hair, clothes, and hugged the flower girl. No cold fingers or businessman's grip about her.

Warm and vital and gorgeous and classy...and so damn sexy.

Jesus. He'd counted on a few days of sun, sand and water. He hadn't counted on her.

It felt like getting shot in the gut again.

Books by the Author

AGAINST THE WIND (2012). Florida Sands Romantic Suspense, Book 1.

JUST ONE LOOK (2014). Florida Sands Romantic Suspense, Book 2.

TAKE A CHANCE ON ME (2016). Florida Sands Romantic Suspense, Book 3.

DANCING IN THE DARK (2013). Shadow Heroes, Book 1.

IN THE ARMS OF A STRANGER (2016). Shadow Heroes, Book 2.

CPSIA information can be obtained
at www.ICGtesting.com
Printed in the USA
LVHW041708250719
625347LV00014B/583/P